Erin and Sam had a past that bound them, that taunted them.

Because so much had never happened.

Little Sara suddenly slipped between them, grabbing their hands and interrrupting Erin's silent stroll down memory lane.

Erin smiled down at the four-year-old and tried to act normal. But how could she? It was happening again.

She couldn't ignore the feelings, old and new, that she harbored for Sam Stone. Even as fears and doubts warned her to stop, to stay away from him, she already felt connected to his daughter, Sara. And if she took the next step, if Sam became as important as his child had…

No, Erin vowed. She couldn't allow that.

She wouldn't….

Dear Reader,

Welcome to Silhouette **Special Edition**...welcome to romance. This month's six wonderful books are guaranteed to become some of your all-time favorites!

Our THAT SPECIAL WOMAN! title for March is *The Sultan's Wives* by Tracy Sinclair. An ambitious photojournalist gets herself in a predicament—the middle of a harem—when she goes in search of a hot story in an exotic land. And she finds that only the fascinating and handsome sultan can get her out of it.

This month Andrea Edwards's new series, THIS TIME, FOREVER, returns with another compelling story of predestined love in *A Rose and A Wedding Vow*. And don't miss *Baby My Baby* by Victoria Pade, as she tells the next tale of the Heller clan siblings from her series A RANCHING FAMILY.

Jake's Mountain by Christine Flynn, a spin-off to her last Special Edition title, *When Morning Comes*, rounds out the month, along with Jennifer Mikels's *Sara's Father* and *The Mother of His Child* by Ann Howard White, a new author to Special Edition.

I hope you enjoy these books, and all the stories to come!

Sincerely,

Tara Gavin
Senior Editor

Please address questions and book requests to:
Silhouette Reader Service
U.S.: 3010 Walden Ave., P.O. Box 1325, Buffalo, NY 14269
Canadian: P.O. Box 609, Fort Erie, Ont. L2A 5X3

JENNIFER MIKELS

SARA'S FATHER

Published by Silhouette Books
America's Publisher of Contemporary Romance

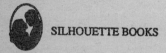 SILHOUETTE BOOKS

ISBN 0-373-09947-9

SARA'S FATHER

Copyright © 1995 by Suzanne Kuhlin

Printed in U.S.A.

Books by Jennifer Mikels

Silhouette Special Edition

A Sporting Affair #66
Whirlwind #124
Remember the Daffodils #478
Double Identity #521
Stargazer #574
Freedom's Just Another Word #623
A Real Charmer #694
A Job for Jack #735
Your Child, My Child #807
Denver's Lady #870
Jake Ryker's Back in Town #929
Sara's Father #947

Silhouette Romance

Lady of the West #462
Maverick #487
Perfect Partners #511
The Bewitching Hour #551

JENNIFER MIKELS

started out as an avid fan of historical novels, which eventually led her to contemporary romances, which in turn led her to try her hand at penning her own novels. She quickly found she preferred romance fiction with its happy endings to the technical writing she had done for a public-relations firm. Between writing and raising two boys, the Phoenix-based author has little time left for hobbies, though she does enjoy cross-country skiing and antique shopping with her husband.

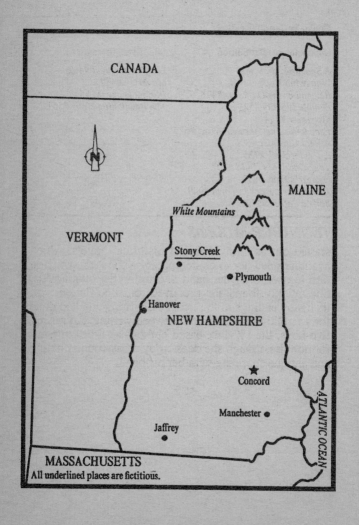

CANADA

VERMONT

MAINE

White Mountains

Stony Creek

Plymouth

Hanover

NEW HAMPSHIRE

Concord

Manchester

Jaffrey

ATLANTIC OCEAN

MASSACHUSETTS
All underlined places are fictitious.

Chapter One

What would she say to him? Nervousness skittered through Erin Delaney as she punched out a phone number. The last time she'd talked to Sam Stone had been at Jill's funeral. Although they'd had a sympathetic exchange, their words had been strained. She'd lost a sister; he'd lost a wife.

At one time, they'd been good friends. At one time, she'd yearned to be closer to him. That hadn't happened, but surely the friendship they'd shared still mattered.

Erin closed her eyes, coiling the telephone cord around her finger, praying that she wasn't making a mistake calling him, that he didn't feel so alienated from her family that he'd refuse to help.

Seconds ticked away before she heard his hello. "Sam, it's Erin." Silence answered her. She couldn't allow anxiousness to gain control of her. Quickly she gathered her thoughts. An inane comment about it being a long time since they'd talked seemed ridiculous. Stumped for an easy way to tell him about her dilemma, she said the only words she could say. "I need you, Sam."

The voice that finally responded was threaded with equal amounts of curiosity and wariness. "Are you calling from New York?"

"Here," she said quickly. "I'm in New Hampshire."

Again, silence. This time she'd expected a question. When he didn't ask why she was calling him, she went on, "Sam, we've got a problem. I'm at the county jail. Rory's in trouble." Panic threatening, she drew a calming breath. "My brother needs a lawyer. Can you come?"

There was no hesitation this time. "I'll be there," he answered.

For a long moment after her goodbye, Sam listened to the dial tone. She's only asking for your help, he reminded himself. Nothing more.

"I thought you might like some coffee." Dorothy Pritchard stood in the doorway with a tray bearing a small coffeepot and a cup.

"Thanks." Sam divided his attention between Dorothy and his four-year-old daughter, who bounded from the floor, presented him with her latest drawing, then plopped back down on the rug.

Hunched forward on the wing chair behind his desk, Sam smiled down at the paper filled with his daughter's impression of colorful butterflies.

"Sara, it's time for bed, isn't it?" Dorothy asked in a soft, sandpapery voice.

Several years ago, Dorothy had retired from teaching. Without being asked, she'd shown up at Sam's door the morning after he'd moved back to town from Boston and had announced that a man alone with a child needed help. Uncertain he'd made the right decision to raise Sara in Stony Creek, he'd hugged the woman. She'd been his freshman history teacher in high school, a firm disciplinarian who'd challenged his mind and had endured his flirtations with every girl in the classroom. A small woman with ample hips, she'd become his right hand, answering phones, keeping his appointments straight and loving his daughter. He couldn't have asked for more.

Her legs tucked beneath her, Sara held a red crayon in midair and sent him an appealing look. "I'm not tired yet."

"It's time."

"Will you finish reading the story?" She yawned while picking up the crayons and putting them back into the box.

"I can't, honey. I have to go somewhere." He shifted a look at Dorothy. "Could you stick around?"

"I can do better. I can finish that story," she said as encouragement to motivate Sara to go to bed.

Sam gave her a thank-you smile. "The train is almost up the hill for the last time," he said about the book he'd been reading to Sara at bedtime.

"And it's chugging, and it's chugging, and it's chugging," Sara announced emphatically.

"It must be tired," Dorothy said.

"It can't be tired," Sara answered with absolute certainty. "It can't stop until it gets up the hill."

"Well, you'll just have to hurry up then so we can read that book."

"I will." She scrambled to a stand and rushed to Sam. With her little arms wrapped tight around his neck, she smacked a wet kiss on his cheek. "Good night, Daddy."

Lightly he ran a hand over her dark shiny hair and gave her an extra squeeze. The bedtime ritual was special to him, the time he spent reading a book to her was soothing, reminding him of what was most worthwhile in his life. But he'd heard a plea, a desperation in Erin's voice. "Tomorrow night we'll start a new book."

"I'll pick out one before I go to bed," she assured him on another yawn.

"Don't forget to brush your teeth."

Trotting toward the door, she lifted her chin to a regal angle. "I always do it."

"I'll come up with you and help you wash your hair," Dorothy said.

"I can do it all by myself."

Shaking his head, Sam laughed. "And all the soap will still be in it."

"I'll help her with that." Dorothy stalled at the door. "New client?"

Sam gathered papers on his desk. "I'm not sure yet. Or how late I'll be. Could you spend the night?"

"Of course." She cackled softly. "I can't tell you how many women in this town would trade places with me to hear you say that to them." Looking amused, she collected Sara's jacket and hat from a nearby chair. "Who's the prospective client who's too impatient to wait until morning?"

"Rory Delaney." Sam swept a cursory glance over the contract he'd been working on. "His sister called," he said as dispassionately as possible.

"Erin?" Pleasure crinkled small lines at the corners of Dorothy's eyes. "She was a favorite of mine."

Sam guessed why. "Because she was smart."

"Yes, and not a smart aleck like you." Over the rim of her glasses, she peered curiously at him. "Why is she calling you?"

Sam caught speculation in her voice. Don't get any notions, he could have told her. While he and Erin had shared laughter, hugs and a few warm, experimental kisses, they'd never been lovers. But he'd struggled for weeks with his feelings before they'd said that final goodbye. During their last months together, he'd begun to sense an affection for her that went beyond enjoying her company, her humor. He'd recognized the power she had over him, but he'd sidestepped those feelings. They'd both had plans that had promised to take them in different directions.

He could still recall the excited look in her eyes when a New York modeling agency had called her. Some big shot passing through the state had seen her photo in the local newspaper after she'd organized a student fund-raiser for a classmate in the hospital. She had the right looks, he'd told her, and had filled her with dreams of glamour as one of their models.

Always Sam would have regrets, but he would never have to feel guilt that he'd interfered with what she'd wanted. He'd learned from his father's mistake, from his mother's sadness. If you really loved someone, sometimes the only way to prove that was to let go.

Dorothy cleared her throat to snag his attention. "Where were you? Thinking about her?"

A frown knitted Sam's brow. "Why would you think so?"

"She was the only one you dated when you were in high school."

"Not the only one," he said offhand to dodge discussion about Erin.

"Yes." Dorothy pursed her lips disapprovingly. "That's right. I remember now how that glazed look crept into your eyes when Marilee Waylen went by in one of her tight skirts. It was quite clear why you dated her."

"Cut me some slack, Dorothy." He stuffed papers in his desk drawer. "I was eighteen then."

"That's your excuse, I assume." She matched his grin. "Except for that brief lapse in sanity, I always thought you were an intelligent boy."

"I think I should say thank-you."

"It's polite." Dorothy snatched up Sara's sweater from the hunter green upholstered chair. "So why is she calling you?"

"Rory's at the county jail."

"My Lord. Police trouble?" At Sam's nod, she frowned. "I don't believe it. He's always been a little wild, but he's no criminal."

Sam pushed back his chair and headed for the door with Dorothy trailing.

"I'm surprised her mother let her call you."

He looked up from buttoning his jacket. The Erin he remembered had always had a mind of her own, but Sam understood Dorothy's reaction. Since she was like family to him, she'd always been privy to his secrets, including the reason why Kathryn Delaney viewed him as the devil incarnate.

"It must have been Erin's idea," Dorothy surmised.

He'd thought so, too. Bending his head, he stepped into the cold night air. "I need you," she'd said. There had been a time when he'd longed to hear those words from her, when she would announce she'd changed her mind and was staying. Even after she'd left, he'd hoped she would call and say she'd made a mistake. None of that had ever happened.

Snowflakes danced on the night air. A wintry November wind chilled the room whenever the outer door opened. Erin ambled back to her mother.

Arms crossed, hugging herself, Kathryn perched on the edge of the wood bench in the large pale green room of the county jail and eyed a man in handcuffs being led toward the iron door and the cells.

Settling on the bench beside her, Erin draped her arm tightly around her mother's shoulder. This was an experience neither she nor her mother had ever expected, one Erin could have missed her entire life. She'd been born and raised in the small New Hampshire town. No Delaney had ever been in trouble before.

"I wish they'd let us see him." A tall, thin woman, Erin's mother remained lovely with age. A trace of gray threaded the soft dark curls framing her face, but only tiny lines crinkled from the corners of her eyes.

If wishful thinking helped, then Erin would have preferred not to have received the phone call that had sent her sprinting down the airport terminal to catch a plane home. She wished she could ease the dread that made her mother tremble. She'd been through so much during the years since Erin's sister Jill had died.

Erin checked the clock on the wall. Not for the first time, guilt weighed her down. She should have been around more for her mother then. She'd always considered herself more sensitive, but she'd been too preoccupied with her own life. This time, she vowed she'd be here for her and for Rory. "Everything will be okay, Mom."

Blue eyes already watery filled with the threat of tears. "I can't believe they're serious. That they've arrested him." Her mother gripped her hand.

"It's a mistake." She prayed it was. In anticipation of her mother's reaction to her next words, she drew a deep breath. "We'll get this straightened out soon. Sam promised to come."

Instead of a response, Kathryn pretended interest in the vending machine. "I think I'd like some coffee."

A tide of tension washed over Erin. She strolled with her mother while rehearsing what to say. They couldn't avoid talking about Sam. She'd meant it when she'd told him that they needed him. Her mother had to accept his help. If she didn't, if she angered Sam, if he walked out—

No! She couldn't allow any of those possibilities to happen. And she couldn't allow past feelings to interfere. She'd have to talk to him, even spend time with him. The coward's way wouldn't work now. It was childish, anyway. Her sister was gone. She no longer had to feel discomfort about her feelings for her sister's husband. And whatever emotion he used to arouse surely had long since passed. "Mom, Rory needed a lawyer. Someone we know."

"You don't know what happened," Kathryn said coldly. "Your brother doesn't understand. Neither do you."

"No, I don't." At some moment after Jill's death, her mother's affection for Sam had disappeared. "But I was here for Jill's funeral. She was Sam's wife. Mom, he grieved for her, too."

Her lips thinned to a tight, stubborn line.

Erin decided on a different approach. "Rory wants him."

"I only agreed because you said you'd deal with him." Kathryn plunked money into the temperamental vending machine and spoke quietly. "If Charlie Carves wasn't off visiting his sister, I'd have called him."

In Erin's opinion, Rory would have had no chance at all if Charlie had taken the case. Before he'd returned to his hometown, Sam had gained criminal experience in Boston. He was their best hope. And he cared about Rory. That seemed more important to her. "Mom, because he's family, he'll—"

"No, he isn't," she flung. "He was my daughter's husband. She's dead. Now only Sara is family."

Sara. How often had Erin thought about her sister's daughter since the funeral? Though she'd sent Christmas and birthday presents to her niece, she was virtually a stranger to the little girl. During this visit, she'd see her.

It was time now. She was done avoiding situations because they aroused a private agony. She'd learned to accept that other children existed in the world, even while her own child was gone.

At Kathryn's weary sigh, Erin steered them toward inconsequential conversation. "I thought I'd miss my flight. It was crazy at the airport."

A vague smile touched the corners of her mother's lips. "I'm glad you're here." She handed Erin a foam cup. "But are you sure you can be away for a while?"

"New York isn't going anywhere."

"What about your modeling assignments?"

"I finished a commercial last week." Deliberately Erin strived for humor, tipping her head. "Shampoo."

They passed time, alternating between her mother filling her in on local gossip and Erin sharing anecdotes from her latest trip to Europe.

And they stared at the clock.

Seconds dragged by, but for Erin, years tumbled back to a more carefree time, days filled with laughter, greasy hamburgers, football games, school dances and Sam smiling at her, holding her close, kissing her.

He'd been her first boyfriend, he'd been the one person she'd have given up everything for. Only he'd never asked.

A blast of cold wind and rushing snow accompanied Sam's dash from the car. Tucking his chin toward his chest, he skirted a snowdrift and climbed the slick steps of the county jail building.

As the warmth of it welcomed him, he stamped snow-crusted boots on a mat, then unbuttoned his jacket. His fingers stilled on the bottom button as he lifted his head and stared at her.

Tall, willowy, she frowned down at the scuffed tile floor as if weighty troubles burdened her shoulders. Raven hair, still shiny, still long, brushed her back with the turn of her head. Gold hoop earrings glittered beneath the overhead lights.

Standing with her, Kathryn held her back ramrod straight. Moments spent with her promised discomfort. Harsh words had passed from her lips to him since he'd moved back to town. He'd taken them as if they were punishment due. For Rory's sake, he would endure more of them.

And for Erin.

"Rude." It had been the first word Erin had ever said to him. Sitting in the school library, bored with reading the mandatory literature about the state's constitution, he'd been making a move on Gloria Keyes, when a reed-thin brunette had stormed up to their table and had rifled that word at him. Her thin arm stretched out, she'd pointed at a sign. "Can you read? It says Silence."

Amused, he'd grinned. Head high, she'd marched out of the library. It hadn't been the first time he'd noticed her. He'd lounged on a bleacher during cheerleaders' tryouts and had thought, ironically, that she should be a model. With those long legs and that porcelain complexion, she didn't belong in the small town of Stony Creek.

After the confrontation in the library, he'd dubbed her with the nickname the Whiz Kid and used it whenever he passed her in the halls or in one of the classes they shared.

She'd shown she was more than pretty and intelligent. She also had a great sense of humor, laughing off his jibes, and they'd begun dating.

They'd both been from the right families with prominent fathers who were regarded highly by their friends and neighbors. Everything had clicked. Athletic, she'd liked to hike and swim and ski. More important, they'd liked each other. The problem came when he began to love her. She'd had too much living ahead of her. So he'd never even whispered words. But he'd missed her. He'd missed her a hell of a lot.

Ambling closer now, he smelled her perfume, something more exquisite and expensive than the jasmine scent she used to wear. "Erin."

She swung around, sloshing the coffee in her cup. "Oh, Sam." For the first time since she'd arrived, she began to relax, sensed the rightness in her decision to call him. "Thank you for coming."

God, she was more beautiful than he remembered. A pang of emotion he'd thought he'd abandoned years ago stirred inside him. As temptation taunted him to draw her into his arms, he looked past her at Kathryn. Glowering, her lips pinched, she maintained her distance. "Whose idea was it to call me?"

"Mine." What if he refused, what if he'd become too estranged to help them? The idea of playing mediator between him and her mother didn't appeal to her, but she'd do whatever was necessary. "But Mom agreed to my calling you. I told her that we need you."

Looking down, he shrugged a shoulder, more to relax than as a response to her comment, and noticed her ringless finger. Jill had told him about her sister's marriage, hadn't wanted to attend the wedding. It was the only time they'd talked about Erin. He wished it had been the only time he'd thought about her. "Is your husband with you?"

The question came unexpectedly. It took a moment before she realized he didn't know her marriage had ended. "I'm divorced, Sam."

The news bothered him. Why? he wanted to ask but wouldn't. Too much time had passed for him to intrude on something so personal. At home, he'd felt safe with his decision to come, believing they had each chosen different lives and different people to live those lives with. But ironically, fate had left them both alone. What had Rory told him over the phone about his brother-in-law after his return from the New York wedding? He hadn't liked him, Sam recalled. A photographer, good-looking, too "city" to suit Rory. "Sorry," he managed to say.

"It's been a while," she said so easily she amazed herself.

Questions stirred. If he was counting right, she hadn't been married long. She used to be level-headed, stable, never quick to give up on anything before. Had she changed so much? "About Rory," he said, reminding himself nothing else was his business. "What's the problem?"

"He's been arrested for stealing a car," she said with an abruptness that made her voice sound strained.

Though years of being a lawyer prevented Sam from having blind faith in anyone, Sam viewed Rory Delaney at eighteen as more roguish than criminal. "What proof do they have?"

Nervous, she fiddled with her left earring. "I don't know." More than anything, she needed reassurances.

Sam scanned the room again, this time for a familiar face among the officers. He saw none and sensed a long evening ahead.

As he shoved his gloves into his coat pockets, relief washed over her. In his eyes, she saw the calmness she longed for. His chiseled face, with a slight cleft in the chin, bore a few faint lines. He needed a shave, the shadow of a beard darkening his square jaw. Damp from the snow, his blond hair glistened.

Skiing had always been a passion for him. Once, he'd told her that given a choice, he'd have been a ski bum. She'd doubted that. He'd always been too focused to live a life without direction. She'd seen his single-mindedness on the football field, at a basketball game, during a debate. If he believed in Rory's innocence, her brother would be okay. Sam wouldn't give up until he proved Rory innocent. "We haven't even been able to talk to him yet."

The shadow of concern in her voice brought his attention back to her. "When did you arrive?"

"I got into New Hampshire late this afternoon. By the time I reached home, my mother was hysterical. She called me in New York and told me two deputies had arrested Rory at work before noon. He called home as soon as he could, but Mom said he didn't make sense."

Erin wrestled to stay calm. "You know his temper. He was furious and frightened at the same time. Mom was panicky. If he explained anything to her, I doubt she heard it. When she called me, she was crying, so I don't know any more than that. I caught the first flight I could, and we shared a conversation of denial while driving here. But he's innocent," she said passionately. "You know he's innocent."

Eyes, dark and frustrated, met his. "Easy," he soothed and touched her shoulder, then regretted it. Intervening years disappeared. For a second, he stood close to the girl she'd been, to the one with whom he'd wanted to spend the rest of his life. "I'll go back and talk to him. Go home," he suggested. "It could be a while before he's arraigned in night court."

Unable to dodge the wave of fear for her brother floating over her, Erin clutched at the sleeve of his pea coat. "But he will come home tonight?"

Clearly she was looking for an assurance. Sam offered the best he could. "I'll do my damnedest."

For what seemed an eternity he stood before the desk sergeant, then disappeared behind the heavy locked door to the cells. She stood quiet as if he were still near, wondering if she'd been unfair to him. Selfishly she'd dragged him into their problem, relying on a past friendship for leverage. But if her mother's feelings toward him had changed, wasn't it natural his would have, too?

"I'll never trust him again," her mother said quietly, suddenly near.

Erin avoided irritating her mother. She didn't understand, but it was the wrong time to ask questions. She only knew her mother's animosity toward him had begun after he'd moved back to Stony Creek. Erin assumed she was looking for someone to blame and had chosen Sam. Her sister had been in a car, driving on a slick road. Accidents happen. Sam couldn't be to blame for that, but he'd committed some unforgivable act in her mother's eyes. "He knows what to do. We don't," she said, banking on sound reasoning to get through to her.

An hour crept by. She paced and nursed a second cup of coffee. As if dazed, her mother sat at the edge of the bench, twisting the straps of her purse. Uneasy for her, Erin launched into inane chatter about bookings, about her hectic schedule when in Norway for a magazine layout and about the freezing weather.

Then silence settled over them again.

Of all the possibilities fluttering through her mind, the worst became paramount when Sam came through the doors alone. She jumped off the hard bench, her stomach churning. "Where's Rory? He doesn't have to stay the night, does he?"

"I knew he couldn't help us," Kathryn quipped behind Erin.

"Mother—" Erin said no more as Rory ambled out.

A suggestion of a smile, the first since Erin had arrived, curved her mother's lips.

Looking contrite, Rory opened his arms to his mother. Over her shoulder, he sent Erin a look of relief. "Guess if you came home, you think this is serious stuff." He shifted from his mother to gather Erin close.

She gripped him to her, suddenly aware how desperate she'd felt just to see him. "I've missed you."

"Ditto." In an instant, she realized how long she had been gone. Years could be counted, but there was no measurement for the emotional changes. When she'd left town to search for success, he'd squirmed as any eight-year-old would beneath her hug. Now, the boy gone in him, he tightened strong arms around her.

"They made me clean out my pockets when I came in." Stepping back, he grumbled, "I need to get my things."

As her mother traced his path, Erin accepted the burden dropped on her. No matter what harsh feelings her mother harbored against Sam, he was due a thank-you now.

Pivoting, she saw him a step from the exit. The fact he was leaving renewed worry that he considered any obligation to them finished. Snatching up her leather gloves from the bench, she dashed to the door. "Sam."

Because he couldn't ignore her, he halted and held the door open for her. He'd already decided he wouldn't defend Rory in court. He'd shunned feelings for her for too long to let them resurface now. Too much time with her meant dealing with what had been, what would never be between them.

Barraged by emotions Erin preceded him outside. Crisp night air whipped around her. Huddling deep within her belted beige coat, she descended the steps with him. "I don't know if I should say I'm sorry or thank you first."

He could have assured her he'd expected nothing else from Kathryn. For the past year, they'd kept their distance from each other in the small town. "Forget it. You've got something more important to think about."

Halting on a step, she stiffened. "The charges won't be dismissed?"

"No, you're going to have a court battle on this."

"You will take the case, won't you?" At his silence, she sensed his hesitation. Fear balled a knot in her stomach that he'd say no. "A retainer." She struggled with a leather glove. "You need—"

Nothing, he told himself. He'd learned to be satisfied with what he had. Sara made that easier. But he couldn't stop himself from asking, "How soon do you have to leave?"

A squeak and the distinct click of the police-station door closing behind someone made her look back. With a hand under their mother's elbow, Rory guided her down the snow-slick steps. "I'm not leaving. Not until I know Rory is out of trouble."

He heard the stubbornness and realized more of the girl he remembered still existed. As she shivered, he couldn't stop himself. While she tugged on a second glove, he reached out and raised the collar of her coat.

Looking up, she tipped her head and felt the heat of his knuckles on her cheek. With his touch, as casual as it was, she'd felt a flutter, an awareness, tension.

All the warnings about her faded. Sam couldn't forget the energetic, smiling girl she'd been, the one who'd laugh at herself, the one who'd made him lie awake for hours thinking about her. And staring into her blue eyes, he knew that he couldn't turn her down. "Come to my office in the morning. We'll discuss everything then." He stepped away quickly, cursing himself. He wasn't any less susceptible to her now than he'd been ten years ago.

Chapter Two

Restless, Erin awoke several times during the night. Her eyes closed, she listened to the distant crow of a rooster. For a second, she fought to orient herself, realizing she wasn't in her New York apartment. Stretching, she stared at the silly-looking owl alarm clock that had awakened her as a teenager. In a corner propped on a blue upholstered chair, a shaggy teddy bear from her early youth leaned against a giant stuffed gorilla Sam had won for her at the state fair.

Through the sheer curtains that matched the white coverlet on the bed, sunlight poured over the floor and the beige carpeting. Memories surfaced while she dressed in the room she'd grown up in. Gone were her music boxes, the wall filled with classmates' photographs and the one of Sam and her at the beach. So much had changed. Mostly she had.

As the rich aroma of coffee beckoned her, she wandered from the room. In the hallway, a portrait photograph of Jill hung on the wall beside ones of Rory and her. Her sister had always talked about marrying a rich man, an important man, living in a big fancy house and having a maid. She'd always talked about moving away. Sam had given her what she'd wanted even though he'd always planned to live in Stony Creek.

Had Jill pressured him to change his mind? Erin had never asked her. They'd never been close sisters, too hampered by sibling rivalry. During their few phone conversations, Jill had rambled on about Sam's law career, then about her wedding, about moving to Boston, about succeeding in her own way. And in the meantime, being the wife of Sam Stone had promised her sister a lofty position in town. Happiness had entered her life for a brief time. For that, Erin was thankful.

She strolled down the hall, but her stride faltered when she reached the doorway of her sister's old bedroom. After Jill had married, her mother had moved her sewing machine in. It was gone now. Again, Jill's collection of perfume bottles rested on top of her old white jewelry box, and her posters of movie stars adorned the walls. The room looked as if Jill had never left.

It looked like a shrine.

Colder suddenly, Erin took a deep painful breath and turned away.

Not ready to talk to her mother or Rory yet, she drifted through the living room to a window of the two-story, wood-frame building. Outside, snow clung to the rooftops and tree branches and carpeted the lawns, and blended with the white shutters bordering the windows.

Gone was the wood swing on the front porch. How many summers had she sat on it, engrossed in a book? She loved reading—anything. Labels on cans, junk mail, magazines, good books. Until her twelfth birthday, she'd divided most of her free time between reading and her favorite sports—softball and skiing. In her twelfth year, Joey Collins had carried her books for her.

At thirteen, she'd seen Sam Stone at the lake—without his shirt on—chasing a screaming Marilee Waylen. By sixteen she still hadn't been endowed with the ogling curves Marilee possessed. Tall and thin, Erin had been all arms and legs. But she'd been the girl Sam had taken everywhere. The first months away from him, she'd missed him terribly. She'd ached for the sound of his voice, a second of laughter with him. By then, she'd left town and he'd gone off to college.

By then, her sister had already taken her place.

"Hey, sis."

Erin pivoted away from the window as Rory bounded down the stairs.

"Come on. I'll make you breakfast," he announced.

It was the last thing on her mind, but she followed him into the kitchen.

Standing by the stove, tired-looking, her mother smiled weakly. "You're both up early."

"I have to work," Rory answered while opening the refrigerator door. He appeared amazingly unfazed by last night's ordeal. Erin sensed it was an act for her mother's sake.

"Erin?"

She focused on her mother, guessing by her expression she'd asked her a question.

"What did he say?" she repeated in a stiff, crisp tone.

Erin assumed the *he* was Sam. "He'll represent Rory. I'm supposed to see him today."

"We want no favors from him."

Rory shot a frown over the refrigerator door.

"Tell him that," her mother insisted before leaving the room.

"Is it always like this?" Erin asked quietly when she and her brother were alone.

"Yep." He layered bacon into a frying pan. "Want some?"

"No."

"I am an expert cook," he said in a bad French accent.

Erin sidled close. "And are you worried?"

He blew out a long breath. "Prison blues don't hold any appeal for me. But I keep telling myself I didn't do anything wrong and—"

"And everything will be okay," Erin said in unison with him.

He laughed. "Have to think that way." He took a quick sip of coffee, then offered her his cup. "Mom would worry about the sky falling if it was a possibility. I feel like hell about everything." He paused as if mentally measuring his words. "She's never really gotten over Jill's death, Erin."

"It's not easy losing a child, Rory. Some people can't find peace."

"Did you?" he asked so low that it was almost inaudible over the sizzling of bacon.

She'd come to terms with her loss, but it hadn't been easy. At what point did a mother heal from the anguish of losing her child? Shock had given way to a consuming ache. She'd relied on routines. No, she'd clung to them. She'd struggled to adjust, certain it was the only way to go on. "Barely," she admitted and slouched against the counter near him. "Mom seemed all right when I came home for her birthday in July."

"You breezed in and out." He poked a fork at the bacon. "One day then another day every Christmas. Hell, she had no trouble covering up what she was feeling."

Erin knew he didn't begrudge her her career. The blunt statement was typical Rory. "I'm sorry. It's been hard on you, hasn't it?"

"I didn't say that to make you feel crummy."

She sipped more coffee. It was a thick, dark brew. "I know."

"It's good you're here. Mom—well, she'll wear a hole in the carpet worrying about me. She can use someone to pace with her, especially if—"

"Hey." Erin punched his shoulder affectionately. "We've got your problem under control now. Sam will help."

"Will he?"

She snagged a bacon strip from the ones draining on a paper towel. "Did he indicate he wouldn't?"

"Last night I got the impression he didn't want to get involved. Can't blame him."

Crisp, the bacon snapped between her fingers. "I feel lost. What happened? Every time I try to ask her, Mom just says that it's his fault."

"I don't know. She seemed okay after Jill's funeral, but when Sam moved back here from Boston, she went to see him. I don't know what happened. She changed then."

"What about Sara?"

"She's a sweetie," he said with genuine affection. "Wait until you see her." He laughed. "But be prepared. She talks and talks and talks."

She held out her cup for more coffee. "So you still see both of them?"

"Not a lot." He slid the eggs onto a plate. "Sure you don't want me to make you a couple?"

Stuffing fingers into the front pocket of her jeans, she shook her head. "No."

"You could use some weight." He gave her a slow once-over. Erin didn't doubt that he curled the toes of local girls with a similar look.

"I eat. You know me, I never gain weight." Behind him, the toaster popped. "Does Mom see Sara?"

"Oh, yeah." He presented his back to her while he buttered toast.

Nothing made sense, she decided. "How does she do that and not have anything to do with Sam?"

"She calls up and tells him she wants to see her," he mumbled, biting into the toast. "I guess it's understood with Sam that he'll be gone when Mom comes to pick her up."

The arrangement sounded strained and unpleasant. A friend in New York, newly divorced, managed a similar agreement with her ex-husband. Claudia claimed her kids struggled with the enmity between their parents and the divided loyalty. Wasn't a four-year-old astute enough to sense friction? "Is Sara aware of all this?"

"She's a pretty smart little girl. She knows Grandma doesn't like her daddy."

"Rory, that's not good."

"Hell, no. But what can anyone do?"

"Find out why?" she said more to herself than her brother.

"I set the lease agreement on your desk." Dorothy's short heels clicked on the highly polished wood floor of Sam's office.

Reluctantly he relinquished a daydream about a girl with dark hair who'd gobbled popcorn at seven in the morning, who'd challenged him to bike races, who'd always made him forget the pressures at home.

"Feel like playing hooky?"

"Contemplating it," he admitted. He stared past the expansive veranda with its latticelike ornamentation at Sara making a snowman.

"Daydreaming usually means one thing."

Sam slanted a look at her.

Comically she cocked an eyebrow. "Love."

"Right." Sam snorted. "Who with? Edna's niece?"

"Lord, forbid that," Dorothy returned. "Only you know who you're daydreaming about. I'm not a mind reader."

"I wasn't daydreaming. I was thinking."

Her head bobbed. "Remember, I was a teacher for a great many years, too many to count anymore," she said. "Whenever some youngster was sitting there looking glassy-eyed at nothing, I could count on him making a fool of himself over some girl before the day was over."

"I was watching my daughter," Sam insisted.

With one hand, she set a letter on the left side of his desk while snatching up a manila folder with her other hand. "Is Rory home?"

"Through the wonders of night court."

"And Erin? How is she?"

"Different." More beautiful, he mused.

"Different in what way?"

"More sophisticated," he answered distractedly while he signed the letter she'd set on his desk. He had no idea what kind of life she'd made for herself. His goals no longer focused on proving himself as good and honorable as his father. His minutes, hours and days revolved around one little girl.

"Guess you're thinking again," Dorothy jibed with a smug know-it-all look.

Sam chose to ignore the extra meaning in her words. If he was thinking about Erin, it was because of Rory. All his life, Sam had believed in justice, not only the kind written about in the books lining the shelves in his office, but fair-minded justice, the kind that controlled the conscience of man. It wasn't so much what he'd learned from Rory, but what his gut instinct told him that made him determined to see Erin's brother free of all charges.

And maybe, even briefly, he'd see Erin smile again the way she used to.

Erin managed to eat two more strips of bacon and an English muffin. For the next two hours, she puttered around the house. She even checked the condition of her skis.

Finally, ice skates dangling from her hand, she strolled to the pond four blocks from her house. She'd once considered training for the Olympics. Lacing up her skates, she smiled. She'd been full of ideas, of energy, at one time and totally stumped as to what direction to take in life.

She'd never doubted her intelligence. School had been easy for her. She'd liked challenges and had even played with the idea of becoming the town's first female mayor. She'd never doubted her ability to learn, to grasp anything new. Over the years, she'd taken political science classes, but she'd tucked political aspirations in the back of her mind when she'd turned sixteen.

Cautiously she stepped onto the ice and glided around the pond several times. Since all was going well, she whirled—and fell. Wincing, she pushed back to her feet. She definitely wasn't Olympic material anymore, but then physical activity in her life now centered more around aerobic classes and running through airports than performing axels and salchows.

Rubbing her backside, she shivered with a chill. It was dumb to waste time in the cold, bruising herself. But as eager as she was to know Sam's plan of defense for Rory, she was stalling.

Swiftly she unlaced her skates. By nature, she wasn't a coward. When still in her teens, she'd ventured to the Big Apple. Modeling hadn't been easy, but she'd dealt with rejection and the antics of a few lecherous photographers. She considered herself a fighter. Hadn't she survived one of life's darkest tragedies?

While she wasn't as immune to Sam as she'd like, she believed she could handle being around him. But what about his child—Jill's child?

She climbed in her car. Face your dragon, Erin told herself, praying that seeing Sara wouldn't slam too many emotions back at her.

Within ten minutes, she was parking her car close to a foot-and-a-half snowdrift bordering the curb in front of a massive Victorian.

Icicles hung from the eaves of the house. Outside a side door, a shingle announcing Sam's law office shuddered beneath the wintry November wind.

Erin nestled turtlelike in her coat and fixed her eyes on her boots. Inside the high wrought-iron fence, small footsteps marred the otherwise unblemished blanket of snow on the front lawn. Bundled in a red-and-white snowsuit, a small child trudged through the snow. Humming, she patted a fluffy white ball between her red mittens. Strands of dark hair fringed the front of the matching knit cap she wore.

Erin studied the petite features of Jill's daughter. She'd been so tiny, so unknowing when family and friends had gathered for Jill's funeral. "Hi," Erin called out.

Coming to a stumbling halt, Sara darted a look toward the door, then turned to Erin. "Hello."

She was beautiful, with eyes so like Sam's that Erin responded instinctively to the smile in them. "Are you building a snowman?" she asked, gesturing toward the lopsided mound of snow at the corner of the house.

"I shouldn't be here." She shot another glance at the door.

"You shouldn't?"

"Not in the front." Sara resumed patting the snow between her mittens. "Daddy and me made a bigger snowman last month, but it melted," she said in a breathless ramble.

Erin crouched down to her level. "It's going to snow a lot now, so maybe you can make another big one."

"Are you a friend of my daddy's?" Sara asked, scooping up more snow.

"Yes." That's what they were now. Friends.

"She's Uncle Rory's sister," Sam announced from the top of the stairs. "That means she's your aunt."

Thoughtfully Sara stared long and hard at him. "Aunt Erin."

Serious and studying, her gaze fixed on Erin.

Moving to the banister, Sam offered more explanation. "Remember, the Christmas—"

"I remember." Her eyes sparkled. "You sent the big black doggie for Christmas," she said brightly. "His name is Blackie."

Erin pushed to her feet. "That's a wonderful name for him." At Christmas time last year, she'd been jetting between the Bahamas for a swimsuit ad and Los Angeles for a shampoo commercial. She'd been mystified about what a four-year-old might like. Then she'd seen the stuffed animal. A soft and cuddly, giant-size, shaggy black dog. She'd nearly missed her flight out of Los Angeles as she'd fought the Christmas rush at the post office to mail it.

Sara packed another snowball. "Daddy explained that Santa Claus has helpers, so sometimes other people besides him give out presents. I liked yours a lot. It was one of my favorites. Well, my very favorite was the big baby doll that Santa brought me. But Blackie—that's his name 'cause he's black," she repeated. "He's my second-best favorite."

"Don't you want to say something else?" Sam asked.

She gave him a pensive stare.

"Magic words," he cued her.

"Oh." She flashed a sunny smile at Erin. "Thank you."

"You're welcome." Erin smiled, recalling her brother's comment about their talkative niece.

"The two of you better come in before you freeze out here. Mrs. Pritchard has hot chocolate waiting for you," he said to his daughter.

She scurried to him, slipping her small hand in his.

"Aren't you supposed to stay in the back yard?" Sam asked.

"I needed more snow." She smiled up at him, showing off tiny white teeth.

Sam couldn't afford to let her charm him. "It's an important rule, Sara. Don't do that again," he said quietly but firmly.

"I won't." Her slim dark brows bunched. "I'm sorry. Are you mad?"

Sam winked. "I'm not mad."

Certain all was well, Sara looked back at Erin. "She—Aunt Erin—said it's going to snow some more, so we can build a great big snowman again."

"We'll give it a beet nose this time."

"Snowmen have carrot noses." She sent him a bemused look. "You're silly, Daddy," she added, and with a giggle, she raced ahead of him into the house.

Erin's heart squeezed. It cost so much to come, to see Jill's daughter, and a memory of her own child, much younger, flashed through her mind. "Sam, she's beautiful."

"Good Delaney genes."

She managed a smile. "You mentioned Mrs. Pritchard," she said as a distraction from her own thoughts. "Dorothy Pritchard?"

Sam held open the door for her and let the fragrance of her perfume drift over him. "The one and only." He waited while she dried booted feet on the doormat. Too easily he could lean closer. Wasn't this why he'd wanted to refuse her request last night? Why he should have, he realized. "Pickle-puss Pritchard," he said, using the nickname he'd tagged her with during high school years, "is my secretary."

Erin swept a look of disbelief up at him. "You're kidding?"

Taking a step from her, he responded to the laugh in her voice. "No."

The confusion he felt came through to her. "I always liked her." While he led her down the long hallway to his office, she unwrapped her wool plaid scarf. She liked his office immediately, a masculine room decorated in rich hunter green and mahogany furniture. "How did she end up working for you?"

"She marched up to my door and told me I needed her."

"And do you?"

With her closeness, he nearly fingered her hair. Tied back and coiled in a single braid, it shone beneath the sunlight piercing through the blinds in his office. "Don't tell her, but she's indispensable," he said, stepping away. "Dorothy made coffee." Giving her a wide berth, he crossed to the tray and poured her a cup. "Sugar? Cream?"

"Black." Erin began unbuttoning her jacket. Facing challenges always made more sense than dodging them. Words needed to be said. It was vital to reestablish the friendship they'd once known. Without it, how could they work together to help Rory? And they'd never get past the strain until they discussed Jill. "Has it been hard, Sam?"

What could he say? He didn't think of Jill often anymore. Guilt nagged at him whenever he did, and because he didn't often enough. "Sara has only a vague memory of Jill. In a way, I'm grateful for that."

But what about you? she wanted to ask.

He avoided what he couldn't, wouldn't, tell her. "It's been difficult for Kathryn." He set coffee cups on the table before her. "There was a time when I really envied you."

More than anyone, she understood what he wasn't saying. Her mother had filled a void in his life after his own mother had left. Erin had hardly known him then, but town gossips had speculated for months about why Judge William Stone's wife had left him and her ten-year-old son—and had never looked back. "You used to be special to my mom," she said softly.

Choosing distance, he took a seat on the plush hunter green sofa across from her. "She meant a lot to me."

"Why is it different now?"

"It just is."

She considered pushing for an answer until she met his stare. He wasn't about to tell her, she realized.

He noticed her gold watch. The thin girl who used to call out hello to everyone she passed on Stony Creek's main street had changed a hell of a lot. She lived in a world of designer clothes, exquisite restaurants and high rollers now. "What's your life like?" It was a question he'd have asked her a decade ago if she'd given him the chance. But from the day she'd left town, she'd cut all ties with him. That had hurt, more than he'd ever been willing to admit to himself before this.

"Crazy. Hectic." She made a stab at humor. "I can't tell you how many times I've heard someone disapprovingly say, 'Mademoiselle, you are sweating.'"

A quick smile sprang to his face. "The glamorous life-style isn't everything you expected?"

She thought of all the times someone had said "chin up" or "turn right" to her. "It's an illusion."

"What is?"

"Glamour. It's grueling work with a lot of temperamental people."

"Sounds like fun," he said in a tongue-in-cheek tone.

Humor lifted the edges of his lips. He hadn't changed too much. She was glad he hadn't.

"I saw your first television commercial. Even bought the toothpaste." Fascinated, he noted that her sweater nearly matched the color of her eyes. "What about the modeling?"

"I did more of that when I first started." She sipped her coffee. "I've had a few nonspeaking parts in commercials for shampoo, deodorant, whatever."

The one he was remembering had shown her dressed in white wandering through dark woods. Sensual as hell. He couldn't even remember the name of the toothpaste.

"I'm taking acting lessons at my agent's insistence. It's helped me get more jobs in commercials."

"Is the big screen next?"

She gave a little laugh. "I'd rather retire and open a bookstore."

Oddly, her words didn't sound strange to him as he thought about how often he'd seen her with her nose stuck in a book. "Or you could run for mayor."

She knew she flushed. "You remember that?"

He saw her blush, found it endearing. "I remember." He remembered everything she'd said. Trouble was ahead if he kept thinking that way. Whatever had been belonged in the past. She'd called him with a purpose, had come about business. Nothing else mattered, he reminded himself, noting what he assumed was impatience as she glanced at the clock on his desk. "I know you're wondering about Rory."

Actually she'd been wondering about him. The marble-and-gold clock looked expensive, the kind given to an employee in gratitude. Had it been given to him when he'd left the Boston law firm? "What have you found out?" she asked, drawn back by his stare. "He's been falsely accused, right?"

Determined to relax, Sam stretched Levi's-clad legs out in front of him. "Do you know what they told him when he was arrested?"

Squarely she faced him. "Something about an eyewitness. That's impossible, Sam. You know that is."

It took effort to concentrate. The thin young girl he'd known had become one sexy-looking woman. "I was going to talk to the sheriff and find out more."

"What more is there to find out?" Incredulity edged her voice. "You believe he didn't do anything, don't you?"

"I believe it."

Emotion, hot and passionate, flashed in her eyes. "I don't know who this eyewitness is or what the person said, but—"

Sam prepared for her reaction. "Don Willis."

"Willis?" Erin moaned softly. A man in his late forties, Willis had worked as a security guard, a maintenance man, a used-car salesman, and hadn't held on to any job for any length of time. "He's always been in trouble himself. How could anyone accept him as an eyewitness to a crime?''

''He claims he saw Rory outside Raynor's Car Salesright before the car was stolen.''

''Rory says he wasn't near there.''

He wished he could touch her forehead to ease away the frown line between her brows.

''He was on his way to see Lori Fremont,'' she went on.

''Did he see her?''

A tinge of annoyance swept through her. It was unfair. Sam wasn't responsible for Rory's problem. ''Well, no, she wasn't home. But that's where he was.'' Her voice trailed off, her attention shifting to Sara standing in the doorway.

''I had hot chocolate,'' she announced.

She continued to stand there, watching Sam and waiting for his okay smile. Usually Dorothy ran interference to keep Sara from barging in when he was doing business. Sam assumed Dorothy considered Erin too much like family for the rules to apply. ''I like your mustache.''

Hugging a huge doll by an arm, Sara took his cue and swiped her tongue at the remains of hot chocolate on her top lip. Her mouth curved in a tight-lipped grin. ''Okay?''

''Looks like you've washed your face.''

She giggled softly, then turned toward Erin. ''This is my baby doll. See? The one I told you about. My very favorite.'' She cradled the doll in her arms. ''You have to be very, very careful with their heads and hold them like this,'' she added, demonstrating a clumsy but affectionate hold on the life-size baby doll. She sidled close to Sam and held out the doll to him.

"How come I have to baby-sit?" he asked with humor.

"'Cause."

Dutifully he took the doll and watched her amble over to Erin.

"Can I sit on your lap?"

Erin fought a swell of uneasiness. She'd learned to mask emotion before the camera, schooled herself to produce a practiced smile. "Of course you can." As she lifted Sara up, the warmth of her small body was overwhelming. How many days and nights had she dreamed of a child's softness in her arms? She drew in a breath, reveling in the sweet scent of her niece.

Sara curled closer. "You smell nice."

Erin couldn't resist; she kissed Sara's forehead. "So do you."

Pleased, Sara beamed. "And you're real pretty."

"She's fishing," Sam cut in on a laugh.

Erin didn't need to fake words. "Well, you're very pretty, too."

At the moment, Sam couldn't have given his daughter a stern look if his life depended on it. "I'm tired of baby-sitting."

Sara released a huge sigh. "He never wants to baby-sit."

"Maybe he's out of practice because he has such a big girl living with him."

Sara started to scramble off Erin's lap. "I guess so."

Don't go yet, Erin wanted to plead. Feeling vulnerable, she touched Sara's hand before the little girl ambled over to Sam.

Reclaiming her doll, she returned her attention to Erin. "I go to school. Not real school, but sort of real school."

"Preschool," Sam explained, recalling how difficult the decision had been to let her go. At first, four hours of separation had seemed like an eternity. She was so small, so young. He'd agonized about letting her go. But during the months that had passed, they'd both adjusted. She, more than he, it seemed.

"Yes, that's what it is," she agreed, smoothing down the hem of the dress on her doll. Sara raised her eyes to Erin. "Where do you live?"

"In New York."

Her head tipped curiously. "Is it far from here?"

"Not too far."

She stood close again and eyed Erin's French braid. "Will you be here now?"

"Only for a while."

Sam considered stopping his daughter, but she'd badger him with questions about Erin if he didn't let her satisfy her curiosity.

"I hope you stay. I have an uncle, but it's nice to have an aunt. Uncle Rory won't play Go Fish with me. Will you?"

As expectation shone in Sara's big eyes, all of Erin's concern about this meeting faded. "We'll see," she returned softly, unsure what Sam's thoughts were about the idea.

Sam stifled a smile, aware of his daughter's persuasive powers. He'd been a sucker for them since the first day he'd seen those big blue eyes.

"Good." Seeming satisfied, she wandered toward the door. "Mrs. P. is making chocolate cake for dinner. I'd better help her." A step from the door, she skidded to a stop. "Bye, Aunt Erin."

"Bye, Sara."

"She's a real chatterbox," Sam said with a laugh.

And a charmer, she acknowledged silently.

"She'll tell you anything you want to know." Wryly he smiled. "She's usually shy with new people. But you always were good with kids."

Unprotected and unprepared, her heart twisted. "It didn't work that way for me."

Not for the first time, he wondered about her marriage. And about her divorce. Because she volunteered nothing, Sam considered the subject of her ex-husband off-limits.

"She's sweet." Erin felt the need to say more. He was a good father. Funny, that even though she'd spent so much time with him during their youth, she'd never detected this tender, patient side of him. Time with Sam had been wild, as if she were riding a roller coaster. "I'm sure it hasn't been easy raising her alone, but you've done a wonderful job."

"We both have our grouchy moments."

Obviously he adored Sara, spent a lot of time with her, Erin mused. Standing, she noticed Sara had stamped her mark on his office. A coloring book and crayons rested on an end table beside the hunter green sofa. A child's book was neatly stuffed in between law books on a bottom shelf of the bookcase. A pink barrette mingled with paper clips in a catchall tray on his mahogany desk.

Her gaze flickered over Sara's photograph on his desk. He'd never know that he had the one thing she ached for—a child. She'd planned not to get emotionally involved, but with something as simple as a smile, Sara had touched her. "I'd like to know Sara better," she said before she considered her own request. Because she'd been afraid of being stormed by old grief, she'd avoided time with Sara. But her sweet face, the sound of her giggles, had stirred the first real pleasure she'd felt in a long time. "Do you mind if I come around?"

Soft, bare of lipstick but shiny, her mouth tempted him, made him wonder if she tasted as sweet as she had years ago. "You don't have to ask."

A step from the door, her stride faltered. Not his words, but the hint of softness in his voice wooed her to look back. Time stood still. The tone he'd used, the look in his eyes threw a quick tremor through her system.

He wanted to recapture the easiness they'd once shared, wanted... He didn't allow himself to finish the thought. "Someone might have seen Rory at the Fremonts. It's possible we'll get lucky and find someone who was rubbernecking out their window that night."

Nodding, she stepped onto the porch. She welcomed the blast of cold air greeting her. She needed something to shock her as she felt a flickering of excitement. The emotion surprised her. She'd thought such a reaction to any man had been buried with other feelings one fatal summer night. "Let's hope so," she murmured.

"I'll call you after I talk to the sheriff."

Inwardly Erin sighed with annoyance at herself, and in a quick, unhesitating manner, she raced down the steps.

Sam stared after her. He'd thought she always seemed to know what direction she wanted to take in life. He hadn't fitted into her plans years ago; he still didn't. Closing the door, he decided he could use time away from her, from the way she tied his guts in knots without doing anything.

"Daddy."

He swung around, feeling the same adolescent guilt he'd known at fourteen when his father had caught him ogling the neighbor's sexy daughter-in-law. "What's up, Peaches?"

She slipped her hand in his as they walked back to his office. "Is Aunt Erin gone?"

"Yes."

"I like her." She tipped her head back to look up at him. "Do you?"

"Yes, I like her." He sank onto the wing chair behind his desk. During the past few months, he'd dated off and on. He'd had little choice. Someone was constantly directing an available female his way. But with all of them, he'd weighed the consequences of his actions. At eighteen, hadn't he thought long and hard about letting Erin go, about not telling her he loved her?

He glanced down at Sara, sitting on the rug, humming the latest tune she'd learned in school. He still wasn't an impulsive man. He couldn't afford to be.

I pressed my lips against the wetness, responding,
asking.

His fingers threaded through my hair, holding my
head still while his mouth took its fill of it, as
wrapping me in his arms, he drizzled a promise.

Chapter Three

Sipping a morning cup of coffee, Sam paced in front
of the kitchen window. Why he'd awakened with a
sense of impatience bothered him. Worse, instead of
fading, it was intensifying. With a look over his
shoulder, he noted his daughter wasn't making great
progress with her breakfast. "Sara, you're dawdling.
Hurry up."

Head bent, chin to her chest, she held her spoon in
midair and frowned at Sam. "What's that mean?"

"Being poky."

A pout thrusted her bottom lip forward. "No, I'm
not."

Sam drained the coffee in his cup and grappled for
patience while she scooped another spoonful of cereal
into her mouth. She was testing cereal this morning,

she'd announced. Which breakfast cereal snapped, crackled or popped the loudest was today's big question. She'd deposited three different brands of cereal into her bowl, and with her spoon was now nudging the various shapes swimming in milk to the side of the bowl to keep them compartmentalized.

Her expression intense, she dipped her spoon in the last of the dinosaur-shaped pieces. "This one's the winner."

"Good. Now, let's get a move on, or you're going to be late. Scoot."

"Scoot," she mimicked, laughing, then ran from the room.

Always she awoke bright and happy. If he hadn't been a morning person, he'd have learned to be one. Until she'd started half days at school, they'd shared these early mornings at a leisurely pace. He still missed her impromptu visits to the office he'd set up in his house out of necessity so he'd be around for her, her sunshiny smile as she squealed about a butterfly she'd seen or a picture she'd colored. But all he'd needed was to see her bubbling with excitement when she shared a story about her playmates or something she'd learned to convince him that sending her to school had been the right decision.

The sound of footsteps running down the hallway alerting him, Sam set his cup in the sink and grabbed his pea coat.

"I'm ready." Bundled in her jacket and gloves, Sara greeted him with a bright grin and a little of his own medicine. "Hurry, hurry. Let's get a move on, or you're going to be late."

"Right behind you." At the doorway, he scooped her up and lifted her above his head, stirring her giggles.

She'd been wrong about Sara. While that thought pleased Erin, during her morning visits to favorite haunts in town, a different realization unsettled her. It was Sam who'd stirred up old feelings. She'd expected a trace of them when with him. That seemed natural. She'd never stopped caring about him. At one time, he'd ignited a fire within her with a kiss. Because that had been a lifetime ago, friendship had sounded sensible.

Then, she'd seen that look. One look and her nerves had quivered. No man had done that to her except him. No man, not even Phillip, though Phillip had been her husband, while she and Sam had never even made love.

Bothered by her own thoughts, she returned home at noon, certain all she needed was to keep busy. Carrying a cup of coffee, she climbed the steps to the attic.

For the next half hour, she rummaged through boxes of youthful treasures that her mother had kept for her, and gave into nostalgia.

Squatting beside one carton, she found no escape from what she viewed as a problem creeping into her life. Lingering over snapshots, dozens of Sam and her, she fingered a sepia-toned photo of them dressed as an old West gunfighter and a saloon girl. They'd had fun, clowning for the camera that day during a trip to the White Mountains. They'd always had fun.

Yet, something beyond that had teetered near whenever they'd been together. Back then, she'd thought it was love. Whether it had been or not no longer mattered. They'd missed their chance together.

Descending the steps from the attic, she wondered if he'd learned about the evidence against her brother. *Evidence.* How could there be evidence if he hadn't committed the crime?

With a sigh, Erin viewed her mother's immaculate kitchen. At her apartment, laundry awaited her. Here, she wandered aimlessly with nothing to do.

According to the note her mother had left her, Rory had gone off to work and then bowling as if life were normal. Her mother had left to help with the church rummage sale that was slated for Saturday and would be there until late evening.

If she remained alone, she knew she'd drive herself crazy. Reaching into the hall closet, she found her old winter coat, a green wool that covered her hips and upper thighs. She slipped into it and shoved on the hood, then snatched Rory's plaid scarf from an end table.

Stopping behind it, she brushed her fingers across the blue-and-white afghan her mother had draped across a chair. She'd knitted a similar but smaller one and had mailed it to Erin months before her child had been born.

Memories wavered at the edge of her mind. On a summer night, her world had crumbled. For months she'd doubted she'd ever know happiness again. She couldn't say she had yet, but she was stronger. She'd learned to protect herself.

Her gaze cut to the photograph of Sara on her mother's small rolltop desk. Her dark hair gleamed like Jill's. Her blue eyes sparkled like Sam's. But the smile, sweet and mischievous, that played across her face was uniquely hers. Infectious, Erin mused, smiling to herself as she went out the door.

At three o'clock, Sam ambled into the federal-style building that housed the town's jail, to see the sheriff. Joe Dunn had always been a no-nonsense type of man. As sheriff for Stony Creek and two neighboring communities, the dedicated law officer, now in his late fifties, understood the difference between mischievous pranks and criminal acts. Dunn self-consciously smoothed down the thin thatch of hair at the crown of his head when Sam questioned him about the evidence against Rory. "You want to know what they've got besides an eyewitness?" he asked in a tone that indicated the prosecutor had a solid case against Rory.

Sam perched on the edge of his desk. "Rory Delaney never gave you any trouble, Joe."

"I know that, but what could I do?" Sympathy colored his voice. "I don't think he did it, but once Willis identified him, I was stuck. And the case was out of my hands because the car was found in a different county. The chief of police there thinks Rory gave the stolen car to someone."

Sam read between the lines. "You're not talking about an isolated incident here, are you?"

"No, I'm not. Rory could be in big trouble."

Squinting as snowflakes flew into his face, Sam trudged to his car. When he'd talked to Rory in jail, Erin's brother had played tough guy, shrugging off the seriousness of the offense against him. Sam figured the kid was scared.

Erin was, too. When he'd touched her, he'd felt her tremble. Disturbingly he'd felt a lot more. Despite a decade, a marriage and the birth of a child, he still wanted her.

Cursing, Sam slammed his car door and cranked the ignition. He had no business thinking that way. Hell, where was his pride? She'd left and had never looked back. He'd waited for a phone call, a letter, anything. Nothing is what he got. She'd started a new life, and he hadn't been a part of it. For too many months, he'd waited.

"Coffee's done." Cheryl Weber, now Cheryl Summers, fixed her gaze on the cups in her hands and crossed the sunny yellow-and-white kitchen to the table. Setting a bright yellow mug before Erin, she gestured with her head to the white pastry bag on the table. "I have jelly-filled doughnuts."

They'd been Erin's favorite snack, but they definitely belonged on Erin's, or any other model's, "no" list. But for old times' sake, she dipped a hand in the pastry bag. As teenagers, she and Cheryl had gormandized on jelly-filled doughnuts during regular talk fests.

With an elbow on the table, Cheryl propped her jaw on her knuckles and let out an envious sigh. "How can you eat those and stay so thin?"

"Probably because I haven't had one of these since I left here." Biting into one, she groaned with a look of ecstasy.

Cheryl grinned, punctuating her dimples. Tall and dark-haired, she'd always insisted she was fat but had the excuse of big bones. In actuality, she had rounded curves and a lovely figure for a woman with three children. "You look wonderful," she said to Erin. "But I thought you'd show up in chic designer clothes."

"This isn't chic?" Erin fanned out the hem of her oversize sweatshirt.

Cheryl laughed. "Stony Creek chic." A more serious look settled on her face. "You said you're here because of the trouble Rory's having."

Her mouth full, Erin nodded. "Sam's going to help."

"Still a hunk, isn't he?"

Erin could hardly say she hadn't noticed. "You're not supposed to look at other men. You're married."

"You know the old saying about married but not dead." Cheryl handed her a napkin. "He's considered *the* catch but doesn't date much. Still pining for him?" she teased.

Deliberately Erin took another bite of the doughnut before answering, "We both married others."

Cheryl inclined her head questioningly. "You've hinted yours wasn't so great."

"It had its down moments." Disastrous, shadowing ones.

"Regrets?"

"No." How could she regret a marriage that had given her a glimpse of the greatest happiness a woman could experience?

"Everyone was surprised when Sam started dating Jill."

Erin offered the excuse she'd accepted years ago. "They always liked each other."

Cheryl twisted her mouth as if forcing silence.

Sensing her friend's reluctance, Erin waited challengingly. "What?"

"You know, I never liked your sister."

"Well, she was a brat," Erin said with affection, recalling how her younger sister had constantly snitched makeup from her and pestered her and Cheryl.

Again, Cheryl looked down.

Erin waved the opened pastry bag under her friend's nose to force her attention back to her.

Cheryl mustered up a slip of a smile. "I had a kid sister, too. Remember Lynn, the mouth," she added with good humor that faded as quickly as it formed. "She wasn't like Jill."

Loyalty insisted that Erin dodge criticism of her sister. "She was sick when she was young. My parents spoiled her. That's all."

"She didn't pull any punches to get things her way."

Erin shrugged noncommittally. More than once since Jill's death, Erin had regretted that she and her sister hadn't been close. "That's the past." She peered over the rim of her coffee cup at Cheryl. "I'm glad I came over. I was going crazy doing nothing."

"That's because you're used to traveling in the fast lane."

She toyed with her spoon. "It's not all that wonderful."

Cheryl frowned briefly. "Oh, I can imagine how terrible it is, wearing wonderful clothes, going fabulous places."

"Don't laugh, but it feels great to sit around in jeans and a sweatshirt." Erin hunched closer. "So tell me everything. All the gossip."

"Oh, gladly. My favorite pastime." Cheryl offered her another doughnut.

People had left town, some got married, had families. Listening to Cheryl's tales, Erin was astounded at how little had really changed.

"She's on her third marriage," Cheryl informed her about Marilee Waylen.

Erin returned her amused smile. "Why am I not surprised?"

"Probably because she never dated any boy longer than a month."

Laughing, Erin refused Cheryl's urging to take another doughnut. "No more." She glanced at the clock. "I have to go."

"So soon?"

Erin pushed back her chair. "We'll do it again." Erin hugged her. "And next time, I'll buy the doughnuts."

Ice-glazed trees and a frosty white mantle clung to everything from fence posts to the rooftops of the narrow wooden storefronts. Stony Creek was Currier and Ives revisited. Its six-block-long main street glistened from the night's new carpet of snow.

Shuffling her booted feet through the snow on the sidewalk, Erin raised her face. More snowflakes danced in the air and coated the sidewalk with a slim film of white. In the city, the sight annoyed Erin. She dreaded the traffic jams, the gray slush when the snow melted. In the country, hours passed before a single set of footsteps blemished the perfectly smooth white blanket.

The visit with Cheryl had failed to quell the restlessness she'd awakened with. Inside the house, she strolled to the kitchen and rummaged in a cupboard. Not giving herself time to feel guilt, she closed her fingers over a bag of potato chips. Another no-no. Crunching on the salty chips, she reminded herself that if she didn't stop eating junk food she was going to be blimp size by the time she returned to New York.

Bored. That's what was wrong. She wasn't used to sitting around and doing nothing. With a disgusted sigh, she wrapped a tie around the top of the bag, dropped it back in the cupboard and shrugged into her jacket again.

It took only a few seconds to locate a snowshovel.

The winter wind caressing her face, she rhythmically scooped snow onto the shovel. Air, crisp and almost biting, blew at her face, yet she stayed outside. Not once while in the city had she known this sense of oneness with her surroundings. Was it because of where she was, or because she was doing something besides getting her nails painted or her hair styled?

Listening to the scrape of the shovel against the cement, she wondered where such discontent had come from. Most women would enjoy being pampered and fussed over, praised and ogled. Then she reminded herself that though she worked hard her looks wouldn't last forever.

She'd saved money diligently for that time in her life, yet she didn't know what she'd do with it. Open a bookstore. She'd said those words flippantly to Sam, but the idea didn't sound so farfetched.

Male pride demanded answers. Flicking on the car radio, Sam turned the dial. The heavy orchestration of Wagner with its hypnotic undertones suited his mood during his drive through town.

Unexpectedly, the anger and hurt he'd buried for years were rising inside him. Even if they'd never made promises to each other, he'd deserved more than nothing from Erin.

He muttered a soft oath and executed a U-turn to take a familiar route toward the Delaney house. If he had an ounce of good sense, he'd stay clear of her. He'd only make a fool out of himself if he went to her ranting and raving about letters and phone calls he hadn't received ten years ago. He even sounded nuts to himself. That all happened so long ago, he reasoned. What did yesterday matter?

Then he saw her.

He cut the engine and stared. How often had he driven up and seen her like that, dressed in the same coat and jeans, shoveling snow?

Without makeup, she looked younger, her skin glowing from the chill and smooth as porcelain. Years ago, at the brink of manhood, he'd lusted for a lot of girls. Now he felt the deep curling desire for one woman. It fired a blaze in the pit of his stomach that he sensed might not go away. "You're going to freeze out here."

The wind whipping at her, she glanced back. Grinning, he lounged against his car. He was dressed casually. With distance between them, he appeared no different than he had years ago when he'd stood outside patiently waiting for her.

Unbelievably a slow-moving heat swept through her. Because nothing else made sense, she decided her imagination was making too much of every meeting. With a final look at her finished task, she set the shovel against the porch banister.

"Got any coffee?" Because she hesitated, he challenged, "Yes or no?"

A few seconds, no more, passed. Her eyes met his, saw a dare, the same kind he silently used to deliver when they were younger. Frowning with confusion, she climbed the steps and opened the door for him. "Plenty." Feeling a little uneasy by his mood, with quick steps she shed her jacket, then rushed to the sink even before he'd stepped into the kitchen behind her. "How do you drink it?"

A shoulder braced against the doorway, Sam dragged his attention away from her snug jeans to the milk pitcher she was holding in the air. "Black."

It seemed ironic to her that she knew he loved classical music, burritos and played a mean game of gin rummy, but hadn't known how he liked his coffee. When they'd last sat like this, he'd opted for soda pop or hot chocolate. So much had changed between them; they'd changed. Yet, he moved around her mother's kitchen in much the way he had a decade ago. "You'll never guess what's under the cake saver," she said.

Keeping her in his vision, Sam dropped to the closest chair. Crazy or not, he found himself thinking constantly about touching her—her hand, her cheek, her softness. "What's under it?"

"Pineapple upside-down cake."

He looked surprised. "I thought your mother only made that for me."

"Such an egotist." Pushing her hair away, she grasped at the lightness. "It was for me," she said with a laugh, and turned on the spigot to wash her hands. "It was my favorite."

"Our favorite."

Something kindled inside her with his subtle reminder. She forced a smile that contradicted the tension coiling through her. She didn't want to think about the past, not any of it. "I'll cut you a slice."

He waited only until she settled on the chair across from him. "You owe me a date."

She stilled, the fork in her hand pausing in midair.

"Remember your last words to me our last Friday together? I asked you to save a date for me when you came home for a visit."

How different she'd been then, full of ideas, of dreams, of desire. "It's saved," she said, picking up on his memory. She'd left at the end of May, had planned to fly back in June to see him before he left for college. A call home had changed her plans. It was then her sister had dropped the emotional bombshell on her, so she'd avoided the trip until Christmastime, then had stayed only a few days before returning to the life she'd chosen.

"I expected you to come home. You never did."

The edge of anger in his voice raised her head. "Yes, I did."

"I never saw you."

"Our timing was off." Why did she feel as if she were walking a tightrope? Growing edgier, she hunted for conversation. "Remember that night when we watched that John Wayne movie at your house?"

Vividly he recalled that evening and how close he'd come to making a move on her. She'd looked cute, her hair hanging loose and soft around her face. "I hated that movie."

"You said you liked it."

He wrapped one hand around the cup she'd set before him. "I didn't like it."

Staring into eyes that had become darker and annoyed-looking, she frowned at how argumentative he sounded. "Then why did you watch it with me?"

"I wanted to be alone with you." He said it calmly, matter-of-factly.

Years ago, she'd have died to hear him say that. It made no sense thinking about that now. No sense at all.

"After you left, I asked about you. I always asked about you. Your mother told me everything except what I wanted to hear." He waited for her eyes to meet his. "That you asked about me."

That admission made more impact on her than she was prepared for.

If he was acting like a macho jerk, so be it, Sam thought. "Why didn't you ever write? Were you too busy to think of me?"

Tension rippled up her spine, over her shoulders to the base of her skull. She hadn't been imagining anger in his voice. "Has something happened? Why are you so angry? When we talked yesterday, you—"

He drilled a furious look at her. "Just answer me."

What happened was over. Why was he insisting on talking about it now? Annoyance bubbled inside her that he was resurrecting feelings that she'd dealt with years ago. "You were dating Jill."

Something akin to a sarcastic smile tipped the edges of his lips. "If I count right, you were gone seven months before I even started seeing her."

She felt a tightening in her chest. In all the time she'd known him, she couldn't remember him lying. "That's not true."

"What isn't?"

"I left at the end of May," she said, vexed that he wasn't being truthful with her. "You were already seeing her in June. Competing with my sister isn't—"

His forearms on the table, he hunched closer. "Who said that?"

"Jill told me."

Sam felt as if he'd been punched in the stomach. "Did you think to ask your mother about that?"

Everything had made sense to her at seventeen. "When I called home the following week, that's when Jill told me. She said you were both being secretive because neither of you thought Mom would approve of her being involved with someone in college.''

She couldn't have stunned him more. "So one week I was dating you, and the minute you left, I started seeing her?''

"I realized you'd cared for her.''

Incredulity raised his voice. "Why in the hell would you have thought that?''

"When we were dating, she was younger, she was seeing someone, but you seemed attracted to her. Whenever you came to the house for me, I saw the way you two were together.''

He muttered an earthy curse. "And you didn't care?''

Hurt. God, she'd been hurt. "I understood.'' It was partial truth. She'd cried after that phone call with her sister. It was all so long ago, but at eighteen, she'd agonized.

"That's big of you. I wish I did.'' He released an exasperated breath. "She was your kid sister. I thought of her that way. I never had the family you had, Erin. Rory and Jill—your mother.'' He held his palms out to her. "Everything at your house was what I wanted most.'' Most of all, he'd wanted her.

"Erin, I didn't start seeing her until before Christmas. Hell, it wasn't even a date. We were both at a party.'' A sense of his own foolishness crept over him. How could he explain about Jill? She'd been around whenever he'd come home from college. In between, she'd written to him, called him. He'd known she was chasing him. He'd been flattered and lonely. Damn lonely for another girl.

She studied his eyes for the truth. Because it was too easy for her to check what he'd said, she began to believe him. All these years she'd assumed exactly the opposite of what he was saying. "What does it matter now?" Confused, she rushed to stand, offering her back to him. Behind her, the legs of the chair scraped on the tile floor. She didn't need to turn around. She knew he stood behind her.

Lightly he brushed a knuckle across her cheek. "It matters," he said softly, touching her shoulder and turning her. She smelled wonderful. Felt wonderful. What had slipped away and why? He curbed his anger but felt manipulated by Jill. He didn't like it one bit. "It matters because I was crazy about you."

"If that's true, why didn't you tell me then? Why did you let me leave, not knowing?"

The big question. "Wrong time."

Now, too, she wanted to tell him but couldn't speak. With his hand cupping the back of her neck, her heart thudded harder. Then his eyes fastened on her mouth. Again, with a look, he transported her back in time. She was eighteen again, with every emotion she'd ever felt for him swarming in on her. She felt the thrill again that she'd known right before he'd kissed her for the first time. "A lot of time has passed. Too much time, Sam," she barely managed to say as his fingers skimmed the curve of her neck.

"This time you're right. Too damn much time," he whispered before his mouth closed over hers.

She could have stopped him. She felt the heat of his breath a second before his mouth caressed hers. She'd had time to resist, yet she didn't. Her lids fluttered as a yearning that had begun for him when she'd been a girl resurfaced. As if it had a will of its own, her hand went to his shoulder, and she swayed closer until his mouth deepened on hers.

Firm and warm, a touch desperate as if making up for lost time, his mouth aroused all the longing of her youth. His taste, sweet and flavored with coffee, spiraled sensation through her. She couldn't sidestep it. Warmth seeped through her in much the way a sip of brandy heats the body. Needs sprang alive, needs she hadn't experienced with any man since before her divorce. Like a taunt, the kiss stoked a fire within her.

It was more than a kiss to Sam. With her arms wrapped around him, the innocence of his youth drifted over him. How could he have known it would be like this? All that he'd stopped believing in with a woman stormed him. She was as soft against him as he'd remembered. Though the sweet scent of her enticed him to linger, to fill himself with the exotic, warm taste of her, with effort, he made himself ease from her. Nothing would be the same again. He knew now he'd resisted her softness before because if he'd made love to her then he'd have never let her go. They'd lost each other, not because of fate as he'd always believed, and he wanted the years back.

Her heart pounding, she steeled herself. So much stood between them. Too much. She stepped back, the hum of a car engine turning her face away from his. Her breathing unsteady, Erin barely managed a casual smile for her mother when she came through the door.

It didn't matter. Disapproval tightened her lips and deepened her frown as she stepped toward them. "Erin, I'd like to talk to you for a moment."

Even though she dreaded the expected confrontation, Erin followed, preferring her mother aired her fury out of Sam's hearing. But she wished she didn't feel so young again.

"He charmed you once before," she said the moment they were alone in the living room. "Are you going to let it happen again? Hasn't he already done enough harm to this family?"

Erin inched forward, her hand out to reach for her mother, to touch her. "Mom, he's trying to help us, help Rory," she reminded her softly, hating the strain between them.

"When Rory's clear, I'll thank him. That's all I'll do."

The weight of their conflict bore down on Erin. Her mother was a softhearted, warm and sensitive woman. What had happened to make her so cold to Sam? Feeling helpless, Erin let her hand drop to her side.

On edge, she pushed the swinging door that separated the kitchen from the dining room to find Sam standing in the back doorway. "You heard?" At his nod, she searched his eyes, anticipating anger. Instead, there was only calm understanding. "I'm sorry."

"I know." He saw concern and bewilderment in her eyes. "Thanks."

"For what?"

"For trying."

Her shoulders drooped as tension poured out of her. "I just don't understand why she's so—"

"Take it easy on her," he cut in, revealing more compassion than she'd have expected. "She's hurting."

It seemed they all were.

He turned away, then back, and smiled slowly. Cupping her chin, he let his mouth whisper across hers.

Erin didn't release the breath she'd been holding until she'd closed the door. When it clicked, she stood still, waiting for her heart to quiet. She couldn't let that happen again. She needed to be steadier around him. She was seeing him only because of Rory. That all made sense, except they'd been together and he hadn't told her anything about his talk with the sheriff.

With a sigh, she leaned back against the door. And she touched her lips, still warm.

Chapter Four

Sam couldn't get Erin out of his mind.

Morning didn't help. He awoke thinking about her.

He drove to Plymouth, thinking about her.

He sat through a meeting, negotiated a merger and still was thinking about her.

Ten years ago, he'd turned his back on his feelings for Erin. He'd wanted her, had even considered asking her to share his life with him. When she made the announcement about a modeling career, the fantasy had withered away. He'd sensed he might end up doing to her what his father had done to his mother. His parents had been miserable married to each other because his mother had felt trapped.

Sam had reasoned that if he'd asked Erin to make a choice, he'd have stifled her. He couldn't deal with her resenting him later, maybe even hating him.

So he'd decided to wait. With years of school ahead of him, he'd had little to offer her. He'd designed a plan. Letters, phone calls, time together when they both came home. Eventually when he had his first job, he'd ask her to marry him. It had been a pipe dream. It had ended abruptly within the first month after she'd left. But fate hadn't twisted them away from each other.

And he damned Jill—and himself.

All morning Erin debated with herself about calling Sam. As confused as she was by what she'd discovered, she was more unnerved by her response to his kiss. She decided she would avoid more contact with him. If she'd learned anything during the past years, it was how to protect herself.

The telephone receiver in her hand, she punched out Sam's number. Anything he needed to tell her about Rory could be done by phone. But what about Sara? She truly longed for more time with her niece, ached for it.

Instead of him, a woman answered, the voice familiar and belonging to the toughest history teacher she'd ever had. "Mrs. Pritchard? It's Erin Delaney."

"Erin." Warmth seeped through the phone line. "How are you?"

Erin responded to the woman's friendliness. "I'm fine, Mrs. Pritchard."

"I'm Dorothy now. I won't be feeling like some old codger and having you and Sam remind me that I taught school for nearly four decades."

"We wouldn't do that," she said, laughing.

"Of course you would. You were both devils in class."

"He was, not me."

"He influenced you," she said lightly.

"A little."

A chuckle hung in her voice. "Here I am going on about all that."

"It's fun to remember." Some of the past, she mused. "Is Sam home?"

"No, he's not. You're calling about Rory?" She clucked her tongue. "I'm sorry about all the trouble he's having."

"Thank you, Mrs.—Dorothy," she corrected herself.

"I don't know when he'll be home. He's in Plymouth on business."

Erin saw an opportunity for one-on-one time with her niece. "Is Sara home?"

"Yes, she is. Do you want to talk to her?"

"No, but I mentioned to Sam that I'd like to visit her. Is it all right if I come now?"

"Of course it is. She'll be delighted to see you. All she talked about was her Aunt Erin when I picked her up from school."

Pleasure swept through her that her niece had accepted her. "I'll be right over."

* * *

"I already started one." Sara proudly pointed then pulled Erin toward the base of a snowman.

Almost physically, Erin felt her heart opening.

Her nose red, Dorothy rolled her eyes. "She wanted to start this after last night's snowfall. Like her father," Dorothy said softly and conspiratorially. "When her mind's made up, little changes it."

Erin touched Dorothy's shoulder. While Sam had gone head-to-head with the challenging history teacher, Erin had truly liked her. "It's wonderful seeing you again."

"And you. And I'll even forgive you for all your shenanigans in my class if you're here to take over building the snowman." Longingly she glanced at the house as if eager to escape to its warmth. "You will, won't you?"

"My pleasure."

"If you get too cold, come in. I'll make coffee," she said, already climbing the back stairs.

"See?" Sara tugged on Erin's hand, drawing her closer to the large ball of snow. She gave Erin a dimpled grin. "I can't put his head on. I'm too short."

"Then it's good I came." Kneeling and working side by side with her, Erin asked, "Do you like school?"

Tilting her head in the way of an artist judging his masterpiece, Sara pushed more snow at the base of the snowman. "A whole lot. Yesterday, Billy Newman got in trouble for hitting. He shouldn't do that," she said, deadly serious.

"No, he shouldn't."

"I made a card for Daddy for Thanksgiving." Interrupting her concentration on the snowman, she shook her head at Erin. "Don't tell him. It's a surprise."

"Oh, I won't. He'll like that."

She nodded agreeably, her hands smoothing out the lumps on the huge ball. "Stephie Lewis went to the dentist and had three cavities," she went on. "He told her to drink lots of milk and water 'cause her teeth are brown back here." She stopped patting the snowman to jam her snow-covered mittened hand in the general direction of her back teeth. Wrinkling her nose, she shook her little shoulders. "Yuk."

Erin stifled a laugh, certain this was an extremely serious conversation. "What did you do in school?"

"I can print my name. And we finger painted today. And we got chocolate chip ice cream 'cause it was Mrs. Rhands', she's my teacher, it was her treat 'cause we were good. And there was a big dog. It's Timmy's grandpa's. And he breathed in my face." She demonstrated by panting. "I'd like a dog," she said wistfully. "Daddy says maybe when I'm bigger. So I won't ask for that for my birthday. Did you know it's my birthday?"

"Not today," Erin said.

Rosy-cheeked, she burst into a smile. "No. But soon." She stared down at the toe of her right boot buried in snow. "Daddy says I'll have a birthday party. I hope it's a big one."

"With all your friends?"

"And Daddy. And you."

Needing contact, Erin brushed strands of Sara's bang off her eyebrow.

"And Uncle Rory." A tiny frown drew down her lips. "I wish Grandma would come, too."

"Maybe she will."

Sara's expression remained serious. "She won't. She never comes here." As her gaze roamed to the street, Erin wondered if Sam was due home soon. "I only see her when I go to her house. She doesn't like my daddy."

"She loves you," Erin said reassuringly. "You know that, don't you?"

Though she nodded, sadness dulled the sparkle in her eyes. Clearly that reassurance hadn't eased her mind.

Erin sought something to distract the child from troubled thoughts. "What would you like for your birthday?"

"I'd like Grandma to come. I'd like her and daddy to like each other."

Unprepared, expecting a childish request for a toy, Erin's heart lurched. There was nothing juvenile in the meaning of Sara's words or the solemn look on her face. "Sara." She wasn't experienced at dealing with a child's worry. She wasn't even sure anything could be done to give Sara what she wanted. Lost for the right words, Erin touched her niece's small shoulders and turned Sara to face her. "I'll see what I can do about that."

"You will? Really?"

She took Sara in her arms. "Yes."

"Promise?" she asked against Erin's neck.

To a child, a broken promise shattered trust. Erin knew she was tackling more than she dared. "If possible."

"Promise," Sara insisted, leaning back with a look as unmistakably challenging as Sam possessed.

How could someone so small drive such a tough deal? she wondered. How could anyone refuse to do everything in their power to give her the birthday wish she wanted so badly? "I promise," she said, and prayed she could keep that vow.

Sara wrapped her arms tightly around Erin and buried her face again in her neck. "I'm glad you're here."

Swiftly, unexpectedly, Erin felt a catch in her chest and kissed her niece's cheek. "So am I."

A block from home, Sam thought about Sara, about the smile he'd receive for getting home early.

When he maneuvered his car onto the driveway, he spotted his daughter on Erin's lap, smiling up at her, their dark heads together. His brain stalled for a moment. To see his child in her arms had an effect on his system that nearly rocked him. Fatherhood had come easy to him. He liked kids; he'd like more. And while he'd never regret a second with Sara, he couldn't help wondering what a child of his and Erin's would have been like.

"Are we going?" Sara asked with bright-eyed excitement, rushing into his arms before he had both feet out of the car.

Nuzzling her neck, Sam stared at Erin. "We're going."

"Yippee, we're going to a football game," Sara sang out. The moment Sam eased her to the ground, she scooted to Erin and grabbed her hand. "You, too," she insisted, jumping up and down.

Erin's caution level rose. It was one thing to spend time with Sara and quite another to be with her and her father. She sidestepped answering Sara. Bending over, she brushed snow from the knees of her jeans. "Have you talked to Rory?"

"Before coming home." He detected her nervousness. "I stopped and told him what the sheriff had to say."

He could have made this easier for her, told her what she wanted to know and let her go. But fairness counted. It wasn't fair she'd intruded on his thoughts all day, had wavered his concentration and now planned to slip away. "Come on along," he urged. "I'll tell you everything."

No was on the tip of her tongue, but she made one mistake. She looked at Sara, her face flushed and glowing with excitement.

"Please, please," Sara begged.

Sam offered his daughter reinforcement. Narrowing his eyes, he delivered his best "we won't take no for an answer" look. "Buy you a pizza. Pineapple and ham."

Sara tugged on her hand. "Say yes."

It was underhanded, she decided. He knew her weaknesses.

Snowflakes rushed down around them, promising sub-zero temperatures before the night ended. Stuffed with pizza, Erin tightened the wool scarf at her neck. "I haven't been to a football game since I left here."

"It's fun," Sara chirped.

"You used to be closer to the playing field doing your rah-rah bit," Sam said over Sara's head as he handed her the hot dog she'd nagged him for.

"That was very important." Her breath steamed on the frosty night air. "It's what kept you guys going."

Amusement laced his voice. "Absolutely." He grimaced in unison with the crowd's groan over an interception. "Looks as if they could use you for encouragement now."

The home team wasn't faring well. By late in the fourth quarter, they were down by fourteen. Erin cringed as their young quarterback drilled another ball toward the end zone that landed right in the hands of an opponent. More groans rippled across the bleachers.

"He's not as good as Uncle Rory was." Sara swiveled a look up at him. "Is he, Daddy?"

Erin blinked against the light flakes of snow blowing at her face. "Your Daddy was good, too."

Sara's eyes widened. "He was?"

"Really good." It could have been yesterday when she'd jumped around cheering, motivating the crowd's support. The only reminder that anything had changed was the excited small child sitting between Sam and her.

"I'm going to get a big head," Sam quipped.

Sara tipped her hooded head back to look up at him. "You're all grown up already. It won't grow anymore. Will it?"

Sam laughed as his daughter's eyes stared intensely at him. "No, don't worry about it."

Her pensive look gave way to another. "There's Tammy." She pointed to a waving towhead a bleacher below them. "See her, Daddy. Can I go down by her?"

"You can go. But stay there."

"I will," she promised, already squeezing by Erin's knees.

Sara passed her in time for Erin to see their team fumble the ball. "They could use you out there."

"It's easier to fumble than you might think," Sam said with sympathy for the young player. A memory surfaced. He'd been a damn good player, but his father had mentioned his lack of skill only after he'd been knocked senseless by two opposing players and had lost the ball. "The judge didn't understand that."

Erin looked sideways at him. She knew his father hadn't been at that game. For that matter, she couldn't recall his father coming to any game. Her heart opened a little because she remembered the real disappointment for him hadn't been on the playing field. It had come later with his father's judgmental remarks after he'd learned about Sam's fumble from town cronies. "He missed a lot of your great plays."

Sam smiled wryly. He and his father had existed in the same house but had never really talked. "Everything was black and white in his eyes. If I failed at something, he viewed it as a reflection on him. It never occurred to him to praise. And he never mentioned my mother. She'd left. Therefore, she was gone."

She wanted him to go on. In all the years they'd known each other, he'd never talked about his mother.

"I know there was talk about another man," Sam continued. "I don't know if there was one, but that isn't why she left."

At the sadness hanging in his voice, she moved closer. "Did you ever hear from her?"

"We had one conversation. She cried, said she was sorry. She'd wanted more than she could find with him."

"Did she find it?"

"I doubt it. By then, her chance to make it big on Broadway had slipped away. I never knew she wanted to act. Sing," he corrected himself. "She had a great voice at one time, visualized herself as the star of a Broadway musical." A mirthless smile touched the edges of his lips. "That image didn't fit a judge's wife." Wind blew harder at his face, making him squint. "I understand why she left." What he'd never understood was why she'd left *him*. He frowned, amazed he'd said so much. Thoughts of his mother never seemed to cross his mind anymore.

Tilting her head, she sensed that some scars from those years hadn't disappeared.

"About earlier?" His voice sounded smoother, softer, dangerous to her. "Did you have trouble at home?" he asked, touching strands of hair flying across her cheek.

She couldn't ignore it. Her face tingled where he'd touched it. "Nothing I can't handle."

He smiled because she sounded so much like the determined young girl he'd known.

Staring at his mouth, recalling the seduction in his kiss, she sensed her own vulnerability around him. Since her divorce, she'd avoided emotional holds, had withdrawn whenever someone got too close. Now wasn't the time to stop. It was time to set him straight. "I told Mom not to worry. That..." His gaze drifted to her lips in the way it used to right before he'd lower his head and his mouth would cover hers. Don't look at me like that, she thought. Don't make me remember the other times when the world was so much less complicated, when just being with you was enough. "That I won't get involved with you," she finished firmly.

"Sounds really simple."

"It is, Sam. I don't want to feel—"

A serious, no-nonsense look, one he'd seen often enough years ago, settled on her face. "For me?" he asked.

Eyes, still intense, met his. "For anyone."

Not for the first time, he wondered about her life, her marriage and divorce, and the man who'd obviously hurt her.

Feeling in some control, she went on, "Years ago, I might have wanted this. I don't now."

He gave her credit for still possessing a steely spirit to meet a challenge head-on. Though he knew little of her past in New York, he sensed she'd relied on that ability to get her through some difficult moments. "What do you want?"

"Your friendship."

He doubted they'd manage only that. "You always had it." It would have been easy to push, but he didn't. Timing was everything.

Noticing Sara standing, then working her way out of the bleachers to return to them, Erin spoke quickly. "I need to tell you something before Sara comes back." At one time, she could have said anything to him. She hoped that was still true. "She told me about a birthday wish when we were building the snowman."

As she reiterated Sara's words, Sam shook his head slowly. "I can't do anything about that one."

"We have to try," Erin insisted. She knew what he wasn't saying. Her mother was the stumbling block to a *happy* birthday for Sara.

"If you can think of a way, let me know." His voice trailed off with Sara's return.

She squeezed back in between them. "Tammy's brother is there," she announced, pointing at one of the players huddled under a heavy cloak on the bench. "He might play." She placed her small mittened hand on Erin's thigh as she craned her neck to see the field. "It's cold." She snuggled closer to Erin. "Aren't you cold?"

Erin curled an arm around Sam's daughter. "Freezing." Lightly she kissed Sara's forehead. There was so much risk, there could be so much pain if she wasn't careful. Yet there was so much to lose if she didn't reach out to this child. She couldn't play it safe this time. To bring Sara happiness, she had to take a chance of getting hurt herself. No, she had no choices. One little girl needed her help.

With the game nearly over, spectators began to file out of the bleachers. Distractedly, Sam returned an acquaintance's wave, then hunched forward to retrieve Sara's hot dog wrapper from the ground. He stilled, caught up in the look in Erin's eyes. He thought... He studied her longer. He thought he saw sorrow. Maybe he had. There was a lot he didn't know about her. "Want to leave?"

Lifting her head from Sara's, Erin mustered an amused smile. "I don't think the outcome is going to change in the next few seconds."

Sara leaned conspiratorially toward Erin. "Will you come back tomorrow to finish our snowman?"

Erin responded with her heart. "If not tomorrow, then the next day. We have to finish him, don't we?"

"Uh-huh. And he's going to be the best snowman in town."

With a knuckle, Erin grazed Sara's freckled nose. "The very best."

Wandering down the bleachers, they inched their way behind Tammy and her parents. Clutching her friend's hand, Sara giggled in between sticking out her tongue to catch snowflakes on it.

While Erin accepted the fact that her niece could melt her with a smile, Sam was another matter. As he touched the small of her back, she vowed to steel herself from the pleasure that he detonated inside her. Amazed, she realized she'd just spent more time with him again without finding out what he'd learned from the sheriff.

When she questioned him, Sam acknowledged to himself that he'd deliberately delayed telling her. He might still have, but her gaze remained unwavering, insisting on information. "The authorities have had a rash of stolen vehicle reports in the past six months."

Erin shoved gloved hands into her jacket pockets. "But Rory wouldn't have had anything to do with those, either."

"According to Joe Dunn, the police believe they're dealing with a car-theft ring."

She tensed at what he hadn't said yet. "And they think Rory is one of them? Why? Because of Don Willis's claim he saw him?"

He saw no point in not telling her everything. "There's more."

Not once during her plane trip or even at the county jail had she expected anything like this could ever happen in her family. They were law-abiding. They followed rules. Her father wouldn't have condoned anything else. "Go on."

"The authorities decided to get a search warrant for the garage where Rory works."

"Logan's Gas Station?" She couldn't believe Ernie Logan, an ex-deputy, ex-councilman, the town's Mr. Nice Guy, would be guilty of anything.

Sam let his gaze wander to Sara skipping ahead of them with Tammy. "No, Rory quit that job about eight months ago. A new garage opened at the edge of town, and he began working there. Ron's Garage," he added.

How little she knew about her brother's life. She'd been away too long, she realized. "Why the search warrant?"

"It's police mentality. They find one thing wrong, they keep digging in case or until they find something else."

Inner tension mushroomed inside her. "And did they find something else?"

He hated being the one to tell her. "They found a stolen engine." Sam kept his voice low to keep their conversation private. "Ron Kale's been accused of possession and selling stolen merchandise."

"But Rory wouldn't—" She stopped as Sam's frown deepened.

"He's been accused of being an accessory."

"Oh, my God." Erin closed her eyes for a second. This couldn't be happening. "So there are two charges against him?"

"Now, listen." He quieted as the crowd thickened near the gates. "Kale insists he bought that engine from a man named Techner."

"Well, then, all they have to do is find this other guy—this Techner."

She made it seem so simple. For the moment, he let her believe it. "Kale had a phone number and address of Techner's garage. But they're bogus, and he can't prove Techner's existence."

And no one believes his story. "What are we going to do?"

The "we" encouraged him. "We're going to do our own checking. We're going to find proof of Techner's existence and his selling the stolen merchandise."

"But that isn't going to help Rory prove he didn't steal the car."

"It will if it's all connected."

"Is that what you think?" she asked anxiously as he offered a ray of hope.

He wanted to give her more and couldn't. "I think it's possible. The operation probably includes thieves stealing the vehicles, selling them for a few hundred, the buyer, probably Techner, dismantling them, removing the parts, selling what he can and abandoning what he can't in salvage yards."

"So if we solve one part of this, we might clear Rory of the other charge."

"And in the meantime, I'm going to check Willis out a little more than the police are doing." He sensed she needed more reassurances. "Tomorrow I'll canvas Lori Fremont's neighborhood. Maybe I'll find someone who did see Rory."

Doing anything appealed to her, but she halted herself from volunteering to go with him. What had been between them, and more, might be only another kiss away.

He caught the eagerness in her eyes, guessed she wanted to get involved in finding out more and wouldn't because it would mean more time with him. What barrier stood between them? he wondered. At some moment in her life, she'd taken on a heavy load of emotional baggage. So for every two steps forward he took, she'd inched back one. "Have you seen old friends?" he asked while they wandered with the crowd.

"Cheryl." A soft gasp slipped out as two boys charged past.

"She's still crazy. Halloween she dressed like a Ninja turtle," he said with amazing nonchalance, considering she was hip-to-hip with him because of the press of the crowd. "Wasn't she the one who lost the top of her bathing suit while swimming at Weirs Beach?"

She grasped on to what she considered safe conversation. She was so embarrassed. "I felt badly that I wasn't around for her."

"Where were we that day?"

She eyed him warily. Usually he had a wonderful memory. She thought about all the fun times they'd shared, taking part in the tug-of-war at the town fair, listening to the babble of an auctioneer, watching the baseball game. She could almost smell the beans baking in the pit. "I think we were playing miniature golf."

As the wind blew at his back, he raised the collar on her jacket. "No, that was a different time. I remember. We were on that cruise around the lake."

Erin didn't need to wonder what he was up to any longer. He'd drummed up a romantic memory.

Sam had intentionally lured her along with him on a lighthearted trip down memory lane, but he remembered quieter moments, heart-stirring ones that had thrown his youthful libido into overdrive. At one time, he'd ached for her. It seemed he still did. "Do you want to go with me tomorrow to talk to Lori's neighbors?"

Erin halted on the sidewalk with him. *Tell him, no,* she warned herself. But her voice wouldn't utter a sound as his gaze locked with hers, daring her to deny what seemed to be inevitable. They had a past that bound them, that taunted them, because so much had never happened.

Snow fell more quickly, dusting her hair and shoulders. A smile warmed his eyes in much the way it had on another day when they'd both been dripping with mud. An argument had led to an affectionate shoving match. They'd tumbled into the muddy puddle, laughing until his eyes had met hers. With a bend of his head, he'd kissed her for the first time. On that day, she'd realized how much she could love him. It wasn't wise to remember that now, but she supposed it was impossible to be with a first love and occasionally not feel seventeen again.

"I'll pick you up around four."

Sara slipped between them, grabbing their hands.

Erin smiled down at her, tried to act normal. How could she? It was happening again. She couldn't ignore the feelings, old and new, for him. Even as fears and doubts warned her to stop, she already felt connected to Sara. If she took the next step, if Sam became as important as his child was... No, she couldn't allow that. She wouldn't.

Chapter Five

She made him feel reckless again, and uncertain. Neither emotion pleased Sam. He knew her so well. He loved her challenging mind, her spirit, her sensitivity, her passion for her family, her natural instincts with children, especially Sara. Yet there was so much he didn't know about her.

Not in the best of moods, Sam hustled Sara through breakfast the next morning. In the car, he felt guilty for being so short-tempered with her.

Beside him, she hummed a song and ran a gloved finger down the window, tracing an *S* on the glass. He'd do anything for his daughter, but he'd been honest with Erin when he'd told her he couldn't give Sara her birthday wish. Only Kathryn held the power of a reconciliation. Nothing he'd say would lessen her pain. He could only intensify it. That was something he refused to do.

"Don't forget." Sara played with the fringe on her scarf.

"What?" he asked as he zipped into the parking lot adjacent to her school building.

"You're not supposed to pick me up at noon."

"Oh, right." Because of the cutting coldness of the wind, he braked close to the door so she wouldn't have to walk far. "Birthday party this afternoon."

"Yes. For Timmy." She unsnapped her seat belt and scooted up on her knees to reach over the back of the seat. "Remember now?" she asked, holding up the brightly wrapped birthday present.

She amazed him sometimes. She never forgot a thing.

"You did forget, didn't you?"

"Yep."

"Daddy, Daddy, Daddy."

Sam chuckled. "Give me a smooch."

Kneeling, she leaned close toward him and planted a wet kiss on his cheek.

"Have fun."

"You, too," she said happily while pushing open the door.

He watched her race toward the white building, its eaves decorated with cartoon characters, then wheeled the car in the direction of the courthouse.

Before four o'clock, he'd handle a business lease, present a developer's plan for a recreational park and have to endure the blustery manner of the town's mayor.

All he wanted to do was see a certain woman.

Midmorning sunlight peeked through the lacy curtains on the living room window. Erin plopped down on the piano bench and ran her fingers across the keyboard. At ten, she'd hated taking lessons and had yearned to be outside climbing a tree or jumping rope.

During the past twenty years, she'd changed her mind. Because she'd learned that music relaxed her, she'd bought a portable keyboard and packed it whenever she'd been on location somewhere.

From memory, she played a song that had been made famous by the pop group Chicago during her high school years. Romantic and lulling, the tune crowded her with another memory. The first time she'd danced to "You're the Inspiration" had been with Sam. Her hand curled around the back of his neck, she'd pressed her cheek against his. Lightly he'd stroked her back. A caress, a seduction, in her youthful mind.

The melody lingered now, though she'd stopped playing. She had to stop this. Emotion, especially love, took so much from a person. What she needed to remember wasn't the way he smiled or the quick thrill from his touch or the heat of his kiss, but the pain she'd survived. She wouldn't be vulnerable again. She wouldn't be hurt, she added for good measure, turning around in response to the ringing of the telephone.

"I thought you'd vanished," the caller said in response to her greeting. Lee Karl was one of the most sought-after and aggressive agents in the world of modeling.

"I wasn't expecting to hear from you." During their last conversation, a quick phone call while she'd waited to take a plane home, she'd explained her problem. "We agreed to no bookings until next year, didn't we?"

"I might have something wonderful," Lee said enthusiastically.

Erin twisted the telephone cord around her finger. "Lee, my brother is still in trouble."

"This won't be until a few more weeks. By that time, you should have everything straightened out there."

She sounded so positive. Erin wished she felt the same. "I don't understand. What's this about?"

"You know that great coffee commercial that features little soap opera segments each time it runs? Well, the advertiser wants to create another one. Not for coffee, but for something else. A soft drink, I think. And they're looking for someone like you. So I'm going to get this going, and I'll let you know what's happening. It's a wonderful opportunity," she said exuberantly.

"What if I'm not free by then?"

Lee clucked her tongue as if there was no concern. "You'll be free. I'm sure of it," she said with her usual iron optimism.

Erin sighed, feeling a little weary suddenly. So much was happening around her that she'd mentally placed her career on a back burner. She wasn't ready to go back to tipping her head, to listening to a photographer's constant prattle.

Sam had stumbled his way through the meeting. He'd listened to his client's grumbling about a cash flow problem but had stared at a Monet on the wall. The painting vibrated with shades of blue, and he'd thought of Erin's eyes.

He'd endured the verbose mayor's diatribe about preserving the environment but had imagined he'd heard a soft, smoky voice.

With a mumbled curse, he whipped his car into the parking lot next to Muriel's Café. A thirty-year-old man, a father, supposedly should have his feet more firmly planted. But his mind betrayed him with thoughts worthier of a lovesick teenager. He needed to see Erin and that made him feel foolish.

Inside the diner, he dropped coins into the telephone and dialed Erin's number. At her greeting, he let out a relieved sigh that she and not Kathryn had answered. "It's Sam. I'm on my way to Lori Fremont's neighborhood. Still want to come along?" Bracing a shoulder against the wall, he visualized that thoughtful, serious look she got when indecisive.

"Yes," she finally answered.

Whether she knew it or not, her acceptance signaled a change. "Then I'll pick you up in a few minutes."

Her nervousness filtered into her voice. "I'll be ready."

Grinning, he set the receiver back in its cradle. Lovesick at almost thirty. He was definitely in trouble. He accepted that little had changed since they'd said goodbye. Again she would leave. But dammit, didn't they deserve more this time?

In disbelief, Erin stared down at the phone. Time with him might be her downfall, but she was tired of doing nothing to help her brother.

She slid on her jacket and a knit cap, then reached for her gloves. Stepping onto the porch, she stared at the heavy pewter clouds hanging low with the promise of a storm. It was the middle of the day. How much trouble could she get into during the light of day?

"Where do we start?" she asked, viewing the familiar tree-lined streets with a tinge of pleasure and sadness.

With her close, for the first time all day, Sam didn't feel torn by distracting thoughts. "With the nosiest neighbor on the street."

When he braked at the end of the block the Fremonts lived on, Erin needed no directions. She strolled beside him up the slick porch steps to Josie Harkins's door. Erin was stunned to see the woman who answered the door had blossomed by at least fifty pounds.

"You're as skinny as ever," she offered as a greeting to Erin. "I suppose you two are poking around because of the mess your brother's in. Knew he'd get into some kind of trouble."

Erin stretched for a calming breath. Though she felt defensive for Rory, she refused to let the woman's vitriolic tongue bait her.

"I didn't see him that night," she said in response to Sam's question. She proved as loquacious as Erin remembered. "Plenty of other nights he was here with the Fremont girl, steaming up the car windows. The only trouble I thought your brother would get into was having Herb Fremont come after him with a shotgun and a marriage license." Her quick sarcastic laugh filled the air. "And then we're all supposed to forget how to count to nine when a baby's born."

A tremble moved through Erin. The woman knew nothing of the facts, yet had already formed an opinion—against Rory.

"That's what happened to the Cooper girl," she went on. "Remember her?"

With effort, Erin nodded politely.

"And Lucie Phillips." Not seeming to notice the cold air, she continued to ramble.

Sam had had enough of the woman's cutting opinions. "Thanks for your help." He slipped a hand under Erin's arm and urged her toward the steps.

"Tell your mother I'll call her," she called out to them.

"She'll be thrilled," Erin murmured.

"It's not nice to lie," Sam teased as their feet hit the sidewalk.

Lowering her head against snowflakes waltzing around them, Erin fixed her eyes on her boots and the icy cement. "Do you think she ever stops?"

"You okay?" With his hip, Sam nudged her to sidestep another icy patch.

Erin slanted a brief look away from her booted feet. "She's hot air."

He accepted her need to make light of the woman's criticism. To acknowledge it made Rory's future seem more dismal. "Be grateful she didn't remember that we were the ones who put the skeleton at her front door that one Halloween."

She sent him a semblance of a smile. "I forgot."

Sam combated an urge to pull her near comfortingly. "You're too young for senility."

"It's selective memory."

"Hey, hi."

In unison, they whirled around and looked up in response to a teenage girl's greeting.

"Lori Fremont," Sam whispered.

Wearing a tight black turtleneck and skin-tight jeans, she reminded Erin of Marilee Waylen. She didn't doubt Rory was dating the buxomy blonde for the same reason Sam had tailed Marilee.

Leaving her doorway, she sauntered to the edge of the porch. "You're Rory's sister, aren't you? Your brother's a real stud muffin." A slow smile that smacked of sensuality lit her face. "But then so are you, Sam."

He seemed to wince, Erin noted.

"Rory said he came to see you last Friday night."

Her gaze traveled over him. "I wasn't home. I wish I had been."

Straining to hear her voice, Sam ambled over to the banister. "Was anyone at home Friday night, Lori?"

Her mouth curving into a seductive smile, she shook her head.

Batting zero, Sam decided on a different approach. "Who lives next door?"

In an offhand manner, she gestured to her right. "Mr. Selds."

"An early-to-bed, early-to-rise type?"

Dark shadowed eyes raised heavenward in a token of disgust. "His lights are out at eight-thirty."

"What about over there?" he asked, pointing to the bungalow on her left.

"The Jorgensens. Mother, father and three brats. I baby-sat once for them." A frown cut a line between her brows. "Never again. The oldest one has a pet hamster that he let out of the cage. They're not home now. They're visiting some relative in Philadelphia."

Sam felt as if he were driving toward a dead end. "How long have they been gone?"

"Since last Saturday."

"The car was stolen on Friday," Erin said quietly to him. "Maybe they saw Rory."

It was a slim hope, but he'd check. "Thanks, Lori." Turning away, he caught a faceful of snow as he looked across the street.

Her voice sang. "Say hi to Rory."

Beneath Sam's guiding hand on her arm, Erin moved across the street. "Why does every boy have a Marilee Waylen in his life?"

"Only if he's lucky," he jibed.

Affectionately she poked him with her elbow.

Mrs. Donaldson, the neighbor across the street, claimed none of her family, which included her and her five cats, had seen Rory that night. Of the pious Enharts, the Mr. answered the door with his hands cupped in prayer and offered nothing except a hope that Rory would repent for his crime.

Sam caught Erin's discouraged look during their stroll toward his car. "Don't forget about the Jorgensens. If they saw Rory, this trip will have been worth it."

Her chin tucked against the wind, she cracked a weak smile.

"Hey." Sam clamped his fingers around her wrist to halt her. Bending slightly, he put his face in front of her. "You used to be more of an optimist. Remember how many times you went back to crotchety Mr. Harbinger's house to convince him he wanted to buy candy to support the band? You were positive he'd say yes eventually."

"That wasn't optimism." Tension knotted her stomach, but she mustered up humor. "I was pushy."

Beneath his hand, hers felt icy. "I'm telling you that we'll get him cleared of this."

When he reached around her and opened the car door, she slid in quickly. She recognized how much she'd needed his certainty, found herself clinging to it. "I never expected anything like this to happen." She waited until he'd settled behind the steering wheel to go on. A frown punctuated her bewilderment. "I suppose I lived a fairy-tale existence when I lived here. This place seemed quiet, so serene, to me."

Sam eased away from the curb. "And different from New York?"

"Yes, but a person can love being in one place and miss another."

He'd never felt that way. During the years he'd lived in Boston, he'd longed to be in Stony Creek, to walk in the woods, to stroll down a street and not see strangers, to raise a family and know his child was safe. "Yet you left."

"I wanted the freedom. I wanted to prove to myself that a skinny kid dreaming of a glamorous life could make it on her own. Everything was too easy here. Isn't that terrible? Some kids dream of a life like I had. I loved growing up here. I loved the people, but my parents were so widely respected that everything was sort of handed to Jill and me. I know now it's different for Rory. He's grown up without Dad running interference for him. But for Jill and I...we never had to work too hard to get what we wanted."

"But you did," he reminded her. "Straight A's. And I know you hit the books." A memory sparked amusement. "Remember the roller-skating date?"

"Oh, I was such a putz, wasn't I? You really wanted to go, and I said I couldn't because I'd been sick that past week and had to study for an exam the next day. I never wanted to get those grades unless I deserved them."

"I found solace in the three bowls of popcorn you made me." In the shadowed light inside the car, he saw the flash of her smile.

"And you watched that awful movie. What was it?"

"*Invasion from Polaris X* or something like that."

She giggled, recalling that he'd fallen asleep on the sofa halfway through the movie. She'd tiptoed to her bedroom and had brought back her pink-and-white afghan.

When he'd awakened, he'd raked a hand through his tousled hair and had delivered a threatening stare, promising to throw her in the icy lake if she'd taken a photo of him and that pink afghan. "I wonder if my mother still has that afghan?"

Sam rifled a killing look at her.

As laughter welled up within her, she was grateful for his effort to stir a more lighthearted mood.

Wasn't this part of what he'd been waiting for? he mused. He'd needed to see that smile, hear the soft, husky sound of her laugh.

Absently Erin watched passing scenery. She could be lured in by more moments of laughter so easily. As he turned his car into her family's driveway, she looked sideways at him and noticed his frown. "Why are you suddenly so quiet?"

"Believe it or not, I was wondering what to make for dinner."

"Dinner?" She yanked off her knit cap and raked gloved fingers through her hair. "Do you really do the cooking?"

"Sam the chef." Looking slightly amused, he added, "chief bottle washer and housekeeper. You name it. If it's domestic, I can do it."

Laughing, she opened her car door. "That I'd like to see."

He rounded the front of the car to meet her. "Come to dinner, then. Join Sara and me."

He grinned in a maddeningly slow way that had never failed to send pinpricks of pleasure across her flesh. His face too close, the memory of his kiss swarmed in on her again. She nearly leaned closer. Nearly. "That wouldn't be a good idea," she said, stepping around him and hurrying up the steps.

Not willing to be ignored, Sam met her at the porch. "Sara would like it," he added to combat her reluctance. "Seven o'clock." He didn't give her a chance to argue. As a lawyer, he was trained to know how much to say and when to stop.

When he was younger, he'd been stubborn to a fault. That hadn't changed, she decided, watching his long, determined strides to his car.

"He's gone?"

Startled, Erin swung around to see her mother standing in the doorway.

"Where did you go?"

"We went to Lori Fremont's neighborhood." Erin entered the house ahead of her mother and swiftly summarized the results of their afternoon canvassing.

"So no help there," Kathryn murmured dismally, moving to the small mahogany table near the door. As if it were the most important thing in the world, she riffled through the mail. "If you get a chance, would you talk to Rory? He's in the garage working on Ed Dohilly's motorcycle. He hides so much from me. I don't know if he's all right."

"I'll talk to him."

They exchanged strained smiles.

With a magazine dangling from her hand, her mother gave Erin her full attention. "He spent the day with Ron Kale calling suppliers. They'd hoped one of them had contact with that man."

"Techner."

Her mother nodded. "I ate a rather late lunch, but I could make you something to eat."

Erin straightened her back. There was no hope for a truce, she realized. "I don't know if I'll be here. Sam invited me over for dinner."

Her mother released a soft, mirthless laugh. "Didn't anything I say matter to you? You haven't been here in years. You don't know what kind of man he is. I do. He was married to Jill."

"I want to spend more time with Sara." She stared out the window at the distant mountains, shadows lengthening across their white peaks. "I want to get to know her."

"Is that the real reason?" Her mother dropped the magazine and unopened letters back on the table. "Remember something. If it hadn't been for him, your sister would be alive today."

Weariness drifted over her. She was tired of fighting with her mother about him, fighting herself because of him, fighting him. "You keep blaming him for the accident and don't explain anything." Erin scrambled for control. She didn't want more dissension between them. Her mother had always been an intelligent, fair woman. The anger she was showing toward Sam wasn't characteristic for a woman who tended to see the best in people.

"Erin, there were reasons why Jill was in that car. It was a terrible night, stormy. She wouldn't have taken off so suddenly if there hadn't been a good reason. Think about that. Think about what he did to your sister that made her run out of the house and get in a car after midnight in such awful weather."

"Did you ask him why she was in the car?"

"He said he had to go out, and when he came home, she was gone."

"That's all?"

"No, he admitted that they'd decided to get a divorce."

"Divorce?" She wondered if she was gaping. All this time, she'd thought her sister's marriage had been perfect. How could it not have been? She'd had everything—security, a home, Sam and a beautiful child. "Why didn't you tell me this before?"

"I didn't think it was important. You have a life now that doesn't include him."

"Is that all he said?"

"He wouldn't tell me more. If someone refuses to explain, then you have to wonder what he is hiding?"

It wasn't totally rational thinking, but how could Erin be sure about anything? Nothing was as she'd thought.

Chapter Six

Confused, Erin looked for something to fill her time until she left for dinner. With an armful of clothes, she ambled into the laundry room. The book she'd taken with her to read didn't help.

Her thoughts straying, she watched her clothes tumble in the dryer. A quivery, unsettling feeling pumped through her as she thought about the evening ahead of her.

She could play mind games with herself and pretend she was going to Sam's tonight only because of Sara. While she anticipated a casual night of listening to her niece's chatter and enjoying a home-cooked meal, was that all she expected?

Uncharacteristically, she slouched on the soft cushioned lawn chair in a corner of the laundry room and closed her eyes. Why hadn't she refused him? Why hadn't she stopped him when he kissed her? Why, when he touched her, did her blood heat?

One answer fit all the questions. Attraction still sparked between them. Foolishly she'd thought she'd be protected from it after all these years. She'd believed he'd chosen her sister. She'd accepted that they had a wonderful marriage.

None of that was true.

Erin shook her head and strolled to the folding table. Although usually a neat freak, she folded a pair of jeans haphazardly, rolled up underwear and tossed bras on top of the basket of clothes. Something was happening again between them, and it scared her.

Grateful for something else to think about, she lugged the basket into the kitchen, dropped it near a corner, then veered toward the garage and Rory. She'd come home because of him. No other reason, she reminded herself.

Electric guitars shrilled from the radio. His back to her, her brother was squatting before a black Harley. Ambling closer, Erin shivered at the cold air blowing in from under the garage door. Crossing her arms, she hugged herself and watched him tighten a nut.

"You just going to stand there?" he yelled without looking back.

"You must have Eskimo blood in you. It's freezing out here."

"It's my warm nature."

With her fingertips, she lightly nudged his head, drawing his laugh. "How can you think with all that noise?" she shouted over the thunderous music.

"Getting old?" he taunted. Pushing to a stand, he yanked a cloth from the rear pocket of his Levi's, then flicked off the radio. "You've got the floor, sis." A hint of unnatural tension edged his voice. Usually he appeared so laid back, almost annoyingly so. In regard to her question about his boss, he shook his head. "I'm sure he isn't any more involved in a car-theft ring than I am."

Erin leaned against his workbench, carefully avoiding the grease splattered on it. Rory was her kid brother, the brat who used to tease her and Jill unmercifully about boyfriends, who'd defended her from a pushy date even though the boy had stood a few feet taller than him. A favor for a favor. She owed him one.

Rory cocked his head and narrowed one eye. "Mom mumbled something this morning about you seeing too much of Sam. Is he heating you up?"

Striving for an amused response, Erin waved a dismissive hand at him. "You have such a poetic way of saying things."

He fiddled with an imaginary mustache. "It's my romantic nature."

She laughed again. "Rory, you're impossible."

"So is it love?"

Life had taught her a lesson she'd never forget. To love a man and a child too much could produce pain as well as pleasure. "We're friends. We'll always be friends," she said as much to convince herself as him.

"Yeah, he's my friend, too. But I don't think we're friends in the same way." He propped the soda can on the lid of his toolbox and grasped the wrench again.

Erin skimmed a swimsuit calendar her brother had tacked on the wall above his workbench. "Why did you think Lori Fremont would be home that night?"

He raked a hand through shaggy dark hair. "She said she would be, so I just dropped by. Too bad she wasn't home." Over his shoulder, he flashed a dashing smile. "For more reasons than an alibi."

Erin didn't buy his "not a care in the world" grin or his casual act this time.

"You never said what brought you here." He motioned toward the motorcycle. "Are you going to trade in that sporty car of yours for one of these?"

She let out a laugh that sounded like a snort.

"No guts, sis."

Probably not, she thought.

"So why are you here?"

"Mom asked me to check on you."

A frown creased his brow. "Try and keep her cool."

Erin rubbed icy hands together. "I'll do my best."

Standing, he draped an arm around her shoulders. "You always could calm her down. I always made her shake her head, and Jill always made her pace."

"Perfect me," Erin said self-mockingly.

"I thought so."

Touched, she felt tears smart her eyes. She couldn't remember him ever delivering a compliment to her. Like all brothers, he'd seemed only to tolerate her. He wasn't a boy now. She sensed an inner strength in him she'd never noticed before. "You've changed."

"It's got to be for the better." Keeping her close, he walked her toward the door. "I think it's called growing up." Exaggeratedly he flexed a well-defined, muscular bicep for her.

"I've decided I forgive you," Erin said, playing along with his light mood.

He squinted an eye. "For?"

"For selling my favorite book."

Groaning, he opened the door to the kitchen. "I thought it might be for reading your diary to my fourth-grade class."

She made a face. "I forgot that one."

Smiling, he slouched against the doorjamb.

She'd always loved him. Now she liked him, too. They'd become friends, she realized.

He took her hand. "Tell her I'm okay."

You will be, she thought. He had to be.

A bag of groceries in his arm, Sam shoved open the back door of his house. With a moan, he scanned the mess he and Sara had left in the kitchen. He hustled to put away the food, then attacked the room. Quickly he stuffed Sara's crayons and coloring books in a cupboard and the kitchen dishes in the dishwasher. As his left foot stuck to something on the tile in front of the sink, he grimaced. It took only a minute to swish a mop across the floor. After that, he yanked out the vacuum and spiffed up the living room, then raced up the steps two at a time and toward the bathroom.

Twenty minutes later, showered and shaved, he lifted a bottle of Bordeaux out of the grocery bag. Candles and crystal might be a nice touch. But this wasn't a romantic dinner. How could it be with a four-year-old joining them? Within the hour, the pork was roasting, the potatoes were browning, the carrots were simmering, and he felt nervous.

Since Jill's death, he'd never entertained a woman. Always he'd considered the complications because of Sara. More often than not, he'd refused invitations by available females. Ones who'd inveigled themselves into Sara's life had earned even more wariness as he'd gauged how much they were ingratiating themselves with his daughter to get closer to him.

None of the guidelines applied to Erin. Her affection for Sara was sincere. He worried more that his daughter ranked first with her, that Erin yearned for more closeness with her instead of him.

Taking a breather from the warmth in the kitchen, he stepped outside to the porch. The coldness chilled him, but he braced a shoulder against the porch upright. He needed to get his head straight about the evening. She'd said *no involvement.* That made sense. As much as he wanted to believe differently, she'd changed. There was an elegance, a sophistication, about her. She lived a different kind of life from him.

But—and it was a big but—when he'd kissed her, the craving had begun. Lust he could deal with. What did he do about wanting to see her smile, to talk to her? When he'd seen her shoveling the snow, she'd looked like the girl who'd always bicycled through town, who'd dressed in a clown's outfit and hammed it up for charity in a water-dunk tank. When he was with her, he forgot everything else. Every time he saw her, heat smoldered as if waiting for the right moment to flare.

He felt it immediately when he opened the door and saw her standing before him. One smile. She weakened him with a simple smile. Snow glistened on her eyelashes, moisture sparkled in her hair, tempting him to touch. "It's snowing again?"

"Just flurries." Nerves. They danced across her skin. Strolling past him, she tugged off her leather gloves. During the drive to his house, she'd given herself a sensible talk. In the past, she'd tackled more difficult problems than she faced now. With a determined optimism, she was convinced they'd find the phantom Techner and Rory would be cleared of all charges. Her mother would listen to reason and attend Sara's birthday party. And Sam would become another memory when she returned to New York. That all sounded so simple and suddenly too much like wishful thinking.

His hands at her shoulders, desire taunted him to bend his head, to seek the sensitive, soft flesh at the curve of her neck. Instead, in a quick move, he took her coat and stepped away. "Would you like wine?"

Breathing had seemed almost impossible for a few seconds. Emotions tumbling together, she drew a sharp breath before looking back over her shoulder. So caught up in her own reactions, she'd been unaware of the distance between them. "Yes," she answered in a steadier voice as he stood at the closet, hanging up her coat. This was a mistake. She already sensed it. Too easily, time with him could erase years. Her only buffer would be Sara. If it weren't for Sara, all resistance might shatter. It was a thought that stirred restless energy.

Hoping for her niece's appearance soon, Erin circled the living room. With its original pine mantel, the room was as she remembered it, but Sam's father's stiff leather furniture had been replaced by a canvas-covered sofa and a chair and ottoman in the same fabric. A rocking chair graced a corner of the room, giving it a homier touch.

"Come with me," Sam urged from the kitchen doorway. "We can talk. I have to check on dinner."

Erin admired an antique chest with a nautical motif and followed him. She thought about her stylish apartment with its loftlike second floor, high ceilings and the dark, classic furniture against the stark white walls in her living room. It was romantic modernism, the decorator had told her.

"It's not Dom Pérignon." Sam poured wine into two fluted glasses. "That okay?"

That he seemed just as nervous as she was tugged at her heart. "Have you forgotten? I'm a chili-dog person."

He could have told her that he'd forgotten nothing. "What else do you like?" he asked, offering her a glass.

Determined to relax, she eyed the oven door and smiled. "What's for dinner?"

"Safe answer. Pork roast." Turning away, he flipped potatoes in the pan. "Sara likes it."

She noted the oven mitt he'd slipped on his right hand. When she'd been with him years ago, he'd played macho man as much as any other teenage boy. Now, he cooked. Her gaze roamed over the immaculate kitchen. And he cleaned.

"Considering how limited her tastes are, it was pork, chicken, spaghetti or peanut butter-and-jelly sandwiches," he added while closing the oven.

And he cared for a child. "Where is Sara?" she asked, eager for her settling presence.

Sam cast a worried glance at the gallery clock on the wall above the stove. "At a birthday party. She should be home soon." He sure as hell hoped so. This wasn't going as he'd planned. He'd wanted more time with Erin, longed for it, but he sensed by her reluctance the danger in steamrolling her. Alone with her, he couldn't guarantee he'd manage to keep hands off. He needed Sara around. Again, he checked the clock, paternal worry slipping through. She should be home. "Dinner's almost—" At the ring of the phone, he tossed the mitt aside and yanked the receiver from the hook.

"Daddy."

A flood of relief floated over him. "Sara, where are you?"

"I'm still at Timmy's house."

"That's a long party," he said calmly, trying to ease away annoyance.

"Uh-huh. And Timmy wants me to have dinner with him. Can I do that? They're having fried chicken and . . . and . . ." As she paused, he could envision her eyes darting around as she tried to remember what she considered important. "Oh, and mashed potatoes and—"

"Did you invite yourself?" he asked before she listed the whole menu.

"No, Daddy, I don't do that."

Sometimes, she did. "Let me talk to Mrs. Bennet."

"Okay."

Sam sent Erin a lopsided grin. "Plans have changed," he told her.

Quickly Ellen Bennet assured him that she'd issued the invitation and would have Sara home by eight. Sam waited as the telephone receiver changed hands again.

"Thank you," Sara said happily.

"Be good."

"Yep. Bye."

Erin gave up her perusal of a bulletin board decorated with Sara's most recent drawings. "Was that Sara? Will she be home soon?"

"No." He took a lengthy view of her in the understated but expensive winter white sweater and pants. It was going to be a difficult night. Just looking at her produced a sharp ache. "It's just you and me tonight."

He made the announcement matter-of-factly, but she was far from relaxed. She returned her attention to the drawings. Each one contained a butterfly, some chartreuse, some purple, some flaming red. She could handle this, she convinced herself. Swiveling around, she let her gaze veer from him cutting meat to the oven door. "What can I do?"

A loaded question. She could stop making his gut tighten, stop looking so damn good to him. He tossed her an oven mitt. "Get the rolls."

Because it helped calm her, Erin concentrated on the task. "You were worried about her, weren't you?"

"Always." He laughed at himself. "I suppose I'll be worse when she becomes a teenager."

She looked up from setting the rolls in a basket. "You never used to worry about anything."

"I wasn't a father then." He worked quickly, carving the meat, surrounding the slices on a platter with golden brown potatoes.

The enticing aroma of pork and a touch of onion permeated the air as she matched his path into the dining room. If she hadn't heard the concern in his voice for his daughter, she'd say he'd planned this.

Within minutes, Erin learned he wasn't one of those people who didn't enjoy his own cooking. Amused, she wondered if he still devoured chili dogs with the gluttony he had shown as a teenager. So much of what she didn't know about him bothered her. While they ate, while they reminisced, while they shared inconsequential moments of their lives in New York and Boston, she yearned to know about him and Jill, about their divorce and the night she died. "You always wanted to come back here, didn't you?"

Over the rim of his wineglass, he grinned. "My father would have said I lacked ambition. He anticipated another judge in the family."

Erin swiped butter across a roll. "And you never had that aspiration?"

"You know me better than that. Anyway, I remember he wasn't around much for me when I was young. I knew when I had kids I'd be different. And living here, I earn decent money, and I still have time to make a snowman with my daughter."

Erin wondered how much of his feelings existed because he was a single parent. "My sister didn't understand that?"

The eyes staring at him were serious. He felt her delving inside him, searching to see beyond what was visible. "Okay," he said softly. "What is it?"

This wasn't any easier than she'd expected. Out the window, snow fluttered like confetti at a ticker-tape parade. "I know my mother blames you for Jill's death. It's not sensible. You know, she thinks that you're the reason Jill didn't stay home that night."

"All wasn't wonderful in our marriage, Erin."

That he wasn't resisting encouraged her. "My mother said something about a divorce."

"We both wanted it." He pushed his plate away. "I don't think we ever really knew each other. That first semester that I came home from college, she was always around. She'd grown up. I was flattered by her attention. We started dating. You know the rest." His last semester at college, they'd gotten married. "When I went back to college, she went with me. We lived on a shoestring that year. After graduation, I was offered a job in Boston with the district attorney's office. I decided to take it for a while. I knew she was happy in the city, and I thought that the criminal experience would be smart for me."

"But you weren't happy?"

"No." He set his napkin on the table. "I wanted to come back here. Right from the beginning, I told her that's what I wanted to do. But because we'd lived so long in Boston, I think she believed we'd stay there."

Erin wasn't surprised. During their youth, Jill had constantly moaned about being bored. She'd always wanted something that the small town hadn't offered. "So you did."

He stared at his hand, at the finger lacking a wedding ring now. "Marriage is a partnership, isn't it? The feelings of one person can't be more important than the other's."

She wondered if he realized that had happened. He'd given up what he'd wanted to keep her sister happy.

Sitting back again, he smiled wryly. "I think she envied you and the life you'd made for yourself. She always wanted excitement."

Erin thought his words ironic. How often after her child's death had she yearned for what Jill had? "Didn't Sara make a difference?"

"For a little while. But we fought a lot." He'd thought he'd said enough, but one look at her eyes, at the message in them as she tried to understand, weakened his resolve to stop. "For a long time, I avoided facing the trouble in our marriage. I believe in marriage, in commitment. I'm sorry I didn't make her happy, but we couldn't find a compromise." She watched the edges of his lips tug upward in a self-deprecating grin. "That's most of it."

No, there was more. She sensed the hard time he'd had with the failure of his marriage, that he still harbored some secret. "There were happy times, though, weren't there?"

"When she was pregnant, I was thrilled," he said honestly.

"Jill, too?"

He saw no point in drudging up what were some of the most difficult days in his life, in telling her about Jill's displeasure at being pregnant. "It was a tough pregnancy," he said simply. "She was sick a lot." Worried she'd see too much in his eyes, he stood and turned away toward the flames in the fireplace.

Nothing he'd said made her understand her mother's attitude better, but she knew that neither he nor Jill had found the happiness they'd been looking for.

"I'm lucky I have Sara," he said, squatting before the fireplace with the poker in his hand. For years, he'd always thought that was enough. Over his shoulder, he looked at Erin. He liked her there, at his dining room table, with a soft look in her eyes.

Erin met his stare, a little too intense, too compelling. Standing, she gestured with a hand toward the dishes on the table. "What about these?"

"I'll do them later." With the fire crackling, Sam replaced the brass poker in the stand. He wanted to bridge the distance between them. She'd been the one woman who could remind him that he was more than a father, that he needed the softness of a woman. But for now, he couldn't take that final step and tell her everything even though he knew it would bring them closer.

Still, every laugh shared, every smile exchanged, had reminded him of a time past, rekindled what was, sparked what might have been, what could be. Temptation rippled through him to take her in his arms again.

As his hands grasped her upper arms and turned her to face him, he set off a fuse of panic within her. "Sam, don't—"

"Don't what?" he asked softly.

Some moments swayed a person's decisions with a force as powerful as a tornado. His fingers touched her chin, angled her face up to him.

She tried not to think about how easy it would be to lean closer, told herself to back away, yet she stood still, waiting, wanting.

Despite what she'd struggled to believe, she wanted his kiss again. As he lowered his head, as his mouth captured hers, she closed her eyes. The taste of him overpowered everything else. Her mouth tingled beneath the pressure of his lips playing across hers, of his tongue pushing the kiss to one of intimacy. Feelings detonated inside her. Weak, suddenly too vulnerable, she placed her hands on his waist, but she didn't push away.

A sweet tinge of longing rushed her to take whatever he offered. Something so simple as his fingers tangling in her hair curled a wanting through her. It ignited sensation.

Youthful dreams sprang alive again. He murmured something against her lips, something that resembled a moan. She didn't need words. With a kiss, he was reminding her of how much she'd once cared about him. She'd forgotten the urgency he could arouse in her. With his hands framing her face, his kiss awakened the desire, the needs she'd learned she possessed—the passion she'd ignored because of where it could take her.

For one breathtaking moment, she nearly surrendered to it. Trembling, she yearned for a moment to slow her heartbeat. More than anything, she didn't want to get hurt. It was a mistake to yearn, to ache, for love that grew stronger every day. If he'd loved her, really had loved her, she'd never doubted that's the kind of love they'd have had. And that was what frightened her the most. No one else but him could touch the heart she'd so carefully protected from more heartache. "No, this won't work," she managed to say between uneven breaths.

"You don't want me?"

He sounded so calm, while her breath trembled. Mad. She was going mad. All she could think about was the pleasure of his kiss. Steadying her breaths, she wrestled for logic. "That shouldn't have happened." Years ago, she'd ached for just this. But now? "That was a mistake," she said quickly.

Lightly he brushed her cheek with the back of his hand. "No." He stared into eyes darker with the heat of the moment. "The mistake was letting you go."

Chapter Seven

He was driving her crazy. It was her first thought the next morning. Last night, Sara's arrival had allowed her to make a quick exit, but was she running from Sam or herself? How could she make him believe her if she kept responding to his kisses?

A shiver passed down her arms. Cuddling under the blanket, she closed her eyes and willed herself to sleep and to stop thinking about him, stop hearing his voice—too soft, too convincing—when he'd said that letting her go had been a mistake.

Eyes closed tight, Erin moaned at the annoying shrill of the telephone. At this rate, she'd be dragging by noon. Grumbling, she fumbled for the receiver before mumbling a groggy hello.

"Morning." It was that voice again, this time sounding much too cheerful. "Did I wake you?"

Cold, she shifted, snuggling deeper under the heavy comforter. "Sam, what time is it?"

"Seven."

She forced open one eye and squinted toward the window and the chilly gray hint of dawn. "It's still dark," she said on a yawn.

"No, the sun's peeking."

"I'm not a good morning person."

He smiled at the smoky, sleepy sound of her voice and gave thought to hearing it in his ear. "I have to be. I'm a father. Sara is Mary Sunshine in the morning. Her mouth moves from the second she opens her eyes. I usually wake up to her singing some catchy tune from 'Sesame Street' or—"

"Sam," she said with an inordinate amount of patience, "she isn't the only one in the family who talks a lot."

He laughed. "Sorry. Guess you're wondering why I called." A moment passed. He'd always been both admired and criticized for his candor. It was eluding him now.

"Why did you call—so early?"

"I needed to hear your voice."

Erin's eyes popped open. Only an insane woman could be in a sleep-induced stupor now. Her eyes wide, she stared at the ceiling. Her mind raced as she searched for something to say.

"You don't have to respond to that." A smile threaded his voice. "Not yet, anyway."

"Sam." Raking fingers through twisted strands of hair, she yawned again. "Sam, what are you doing?"

"Right now, I'm talking to a beautiful woman."

"That's not what I meant." If only she wasn't so sleepy, she'd make more sense, she reasoned. "Why me?"

"There's no one else I want to talk to. But relax, I'm not asking for you to say anything back. No pressure," he assured her.

She fluffed the pillow behind her. If she wasn't staring at the silly gorilla he'd won for her and couldn't hear the ticking of the alarm clock, she'd think she was dreaming. But she wasn't dreaming. She was in the middle of a seductive morning phone call from Sam Stone. She drew a deep but not quite steady breath. "I don't want complications, Sam."

"Hell," he said, offering a familiar-sounding laugh, "let's worry about them when or if they happen. Sound fair?"

It sounded dangerous to her. But she couldn't get a refusal out. "One more thing."

"Anything," he said lightly.

"Don't wake me up again so early."

He laughed more fully this time. He didn't plan to do anything this early in the morning with her from now on except hold her. "It's a deal. Talk to you later. I'm heading for the sheriff's."

Erin struggled to be more alert. "Why are you going there?"

"He called. He wants to talk to me."

"That must mean he's found out something."

He heard a smile in her voice. "I don't know," he answered. He wanted to keep that smile on her face and bring her good news. But if it came, he'd have to face what he'd always known; she'd leave.

"You'll let me know as soon as you're done talking to him?"

"I'll be right over. Good night," he sang out.

She held on to the telephone receiver a second longer and laughed at his teasing words. Did he really think she'd go back to sleep now?

Sam shook his head disbelievingly as he set down the telephone receiver. Well, he'd done it now. But if he hadn't called her, he'd never have gotten anything done today. Contracts, wills, mergers. None of it had mattered until he'd heard her voice. And now that he had, he was still staring at the stack of papers on his desk.

He'd awakened even before Sara this morning. Barely out of the semiconscious state, his first thought had been of Erin, of the way things used to be, of her sitting beside him in his old car, sunlight dancing on her hair as the wind tossed it. Of the way she'd felt in his arms, the sweetness of her mouth. And he'd known nothing between them would ever be casual again. For too many years, she'd lingered in his mind.

Needs had stirred just thinking about her and had made him ease from the bed and plunge himself into a cold shower.

Even by the time he'd had his morning coffee, he hadn't purged her from his thoughts. He'd settled behind his desk to play catch-up with work and had simply stared at the documents Dorothy had typed yesterday. Love was creeping over him. The realization knocked the wind from him. He'd accepted the attraction, the lust, the affection. They'd all been nurtured years ago, but passion alone wouldn't satisfy him. He wanted the time that had been stolen from them. He wanted her in his life.

Rushing because of the cold, Erin tugged up snug jeans and slipped on a heavy blue sweatshirt, then hurried to the kitchen. She felt terribly young suddenly and frightened of breaking a heart that wasn't quite mended.

"Did I hear the phone ring?"

Erin swung her gaze away from the kitchen window and the snow sticking to the porch railing. As she cupped her hands around her coffee cup, steam rose to her face. "It was Sam, Mom."

Predictably, her mother frowned. "He called so early." She paused in pouring a glass of orange juice. "Why? Is something else wrong?"

"No. He called to talk to me."

"I see."

It amazed Erin that those two words reflected so much meaning when delivered with motherly disapproval. Erin joined her at the table. "I talked to Rory, Mom. He's all right," she said, setting a hand on her mother's.

A deeper frown fluttered across her face. "I worry so."

"I know." Erin felt the sweep of her mother's eyes over her heavy sweater.

"You're going out?"

Determined to leave the house with both of them in a good mood, she grinned. "Yes. I'm going to go build a snowman with my favorite niece."

Sam closed the door to the sheriff's office with a thud. A biting wind whipping around him, he muscled his way back to his car and watched the town's snowplow trudging down Main Street. He cranked the engine of his car twice before it revved.

Until now, lack of information had stymied him. He couldn't ignore what Joe Dunn had told him, even if it was a lousy day for a drive.

Stopping at the corner minimarket, Sam dashed in for milk and a loaf of bread for breakfast tomorrow. Tonight he'd promised Sara fried chicken for dinner.

Only one woman stood ahead of him in the checkout line. It was the wrong woman—Josie Harkins.

Though he prided himself on patience, he was beginning to lose it as she babbled to the clerk about her sister's husband who'd lost his third job in six months.

When she smiled at him, he managed a polite nod. A five-minute stop had evolved into nearly fifteen before he was pushing open the door to step outside. His palm remained flat against it, holding it open for the woman approaching.

Unlike other times, Kathryn's eyes met and held his stare. Still, he expected her to pass him without a word, something she'd done ever since his return to Stony Creek. Instead, she paused at the doorway. Hope flickered through him that she might be softening. For Sara's sake, he wanted the anger gone between them.

For himself, too. He'd been honest with Erin about his feelings toward her mother. He'd grown up in a house with a strict disciplinarian who'd believed in hard work and rules but little affection. Laughter was something he'd found outside of the home. Kathryn had filled a maternal void in his life. She'd talked to him; she'd listened. She'd treated him as one of her own. He'd lost more than his wife when Jill had died. He'd lost the warmth and caring of a special woman. "Kathryn—"

"This time stay away from Erin."

Sam stiffened at the cutting edge in her voice.

"She's not interested. If she sees you, it's only because of Rory. And because of Sara. She wants to know Sara better."

"I know that."

"Only Sara," she said emphatically. "She was at your house earlier, not to see you, but Sara."

She moved past him, not waiting for a response.

He didn't have one.

Back in his car, he kneaded his forehead with two fingers. The dull headache nagging at him since he'd left the sheriff's office pounded harder. Despite Kathryn's words, he'd felt something more complex than desire was drawing Erin and him together. Was it Sara? He believed Erin cared for Sara. From a father's viewpoint, he thought it would be hard not to.

But was he imagining more than there was between Erin and him? Lost in thoughts, he nearly laughed at himself as he realized he'd driven to her house almost mechanically. Fool or not, he had to believe, wanted to believe, she was beginning to care again for him.

* * *

All the pep talks in the world proved futile when Erin opened the door to Sam. Her first reaction was pleasure. She remembered his promise to see her after his talk with the sheriff, but she recognized the quick thrill, the hint of excitement, that she felt simply because he was there. "It's cold again," she said, opening the door wider to him.

Sam dried his feet on the mat. "Freezing."

"Have you talked to the sheriff?"

"First things first. Do you have any aspirin?"

She frowned at him, then spun away. When she returned she waited patiently while he tossed the aspirin into his mouth and downed water.

Certain of Kathryn's arrival soon, Sam didn't bother to remove his jacket. Quickly he capsulized what he'd been told.

Leaning back against the kitchen counter, Erin tempered the hope pumping through her. "Let me make sure I understand this. The sheriff said that authorities near Concord raided a parts shop?"

"Right. And they identified stolen parts at it. When they traced serial numbers, some of the parts there belonged to the car Rory is accused of stealing."

"So what we need to find out is who sold those parts to the shop?"

"That's what we need to do." He looked past her at the rushing snowflakes. "But I think you should stay here."

The idea didn't please her. "You're joking."

"Have you looked out the window?" he asked without humor. "There's a damn blizzard starting. You stay. I'll go."

"No," she answered, venting her frustration.

She was revealing a stubbornness he wasn't unfamiliar with.

Erin pushed away from the counter. "Sam, I'm going with you." Her chin up, she met his gaze head-on. "I'm tired of standing around here doing nothing."

As much as he'd like her company, he'd prefer to be responsible only for himself on the icy roads. He considered a different approach. "I need you to watch Sara. Someone has to."

"Dorothy—"

"Can't. It's her sister's anniversary."

Erin watched her mother's car pull into the driveway. "Then let my mother watch Sara."

He wondered if she was losing it. Sam started to shake his head.

"Wait a minute," she said, annoyed with his quick refusal. "It's a good idea. If Sara is with my mother, she might tell her how much she wants her at the birthday party."

Sam cast a look out the window. "Your mother isn't going to want you out in a snowstorm with me."

"I'm not her little girl. I make my own decisions."

He zeroed in on the real reason for his continued reluctance. "I can't ask her to do it."

Of course he couldn't. The task fell on her shoulders. "I'll be right back," she told him, turning away.

Sam bided his time in the kitchen. When he was eighteen, it had been more like home to him than his own. As clearly as if it were yesterday, he could still see his mother leaving theirs. Another image tumbled over that one. Jill had had the same look in her eyes as his

IT'S FUN! IT'S FREE!
AND IT COULD MAKE YOU A

MILLIONAIRE

If you've ever played scratch-off lottery tickets, you should be familiar with how our games work. On each of the first four tickets (numbered 1 to 4 in the upper right) there are Pink Strips to scratch off.

Using a coin, do just that—carefully scratch the PINK strips to reveal how much each ticket could be worth if it is a winning ticket. Tickets could be worth from $100.00 to $1,000,000.00 in lifetime money ($33,333.33 each year for 30 years).

Note, also, that each of your 4 tickets has a unique sweepstakes Number . . . and that's 4 chances for a **BIG WIN!**

FREE BOOKS!

At the same time you play your tickets to qualify for big prizes, you are invited to play ticket #5 to get brand-new Silhouette Special Edition® novels. These books have a cover price of $3.75 each, but they are yours to keep absolutely free.

There's no catch. You're under no obligation to buy anything. We charge nothing—ZERO—for your first shipment. And you don't have to make any minimum number of purchases—not even one!

The fact is thousands of readers enjoy receiving books by mail from the Silhouette Reader Service™. They like the convenience of home delivery . . . they like getting the best new novels months before they're available in bookstores . . . and they love our discount prices!

We hope that after receiving your free books you'll want to remain a subscriber. But the choice is yours—to continue or cancel, anytime at all! So why not take us up on our invitation, with no risk of any kind. You'll be glad you did!

PLUS A FREE GIFT!

One more thing, when you accept the free books on ticket #5, you are also entitled to play ticket #6, which is GOOD FOR A GREAT GIFT! Like the books, this gift is totally free and yours to keep as thanks for giving our Reader Service a try!

So scratch off the PINK STRIPS on all your BIG WIN tickets and send for everything today! You've got nothing to lose and everything to gain!

Here are your BIG WIN Game Tickets potentially worth from $100.00 to $1,000,000.00 each. Scratch off the PINK STRIP on each of your Sweepstakes tickets to see what you could win and mail your entry right away. (SEE BACK OF BOOK FOR DETAILS!)

This could be your lucky day-GOOD LUCK!

FOLD AND DETACH ALONG THIS DOTTED LINE—RETURN ALL GAME TICKETS INTACT.

TICKET 1
Scratch PINK STRIP to reveal potential value of cash prize if the sweepstakes number on this ticket is a winning number. Return all game tickets intact.

LUCKY NUMBER

8W 976332

TICKET 2
Scratch PINK STRIP to reveal potential value of cash prize if the sweepstakes number on this ticket is a winning number. Return all game tickets intact.

LUCKY NUMBER

2A 976496

TICKET 3
Scratch PINK STRIP to reveal potential value of cash prize if the sweepstakes number on this ticket is a winning number. Return all game tickets intact.

LUCKY NUMBER

5Q 976329

TICKET 4
Scratch PINK STRIP to reveal potential value of cash prize if the sweepstakes number on this ticket is a winning number. Return all game tickets intact.

LUCKY NUMBER

9G 981594

TICKET 5
Scratch PINK STRIP to reveal number of books you will receive. These books, part of a sampling program to introduce romance readers to the benefits of the Reader Service, are free.

AUTHORIZATION CODE

130107-742

TICKET 6
All gifts are free. No purchase required. Scratch PINK STRIP to reveal free gift, our thanks to readers for trying our books.

AUTHORIZATION CODE

130107-742

YES! Enter my Lucky Numbers in The Million Dollar Sweepstakes (III) and when winners are selected, tell me if I've won any prize. If the PINK STRIP is scratched off on ticket #5, I will also receive four FREE Silhouette Special Edition® novels along with the FREE GIFT on ticket #6, as explained on the back and on the opposite page. 235 CIS AS2V (U-SIL-SE-03/95)

NAME _____

ADDRESS _____ APT. _____

CITY _____ STATE _____ ZIP CODE _____

Book offer limited to one per household and not valid to current Silhouette Special Edition® subscribers. All orders subject to approval.
© 1991 HARLEQUIN ENTERPRISES LIMITED.

PRINTED IN U.S.A.

THE SILHOUETTE READER SERVICE™: HERE'S HOW IT WORKS

Accepting free books places you under no obligation to buy anything. You may keep the books and gift and return the shipping statement marked "cancel". If you do not cancel, about a month later we will send you 6 additional novels, and bill you just $2.89 each plus 25¢ delivery and applicable sales tax, if any.* That's the complete price, and—compared to cover prices of $3.75 each—quite a bargain! You may cancel at any time, but if you choose to continue, every month we'll send you 6 more books, which you may either purchase at the discount price...or return at our expense and cancel your subscription.

* Terms and prices subject to change without notice. Sales tax applicable in N.Y.

BUSINESS REPLY MAIL

FIRST CLASS MAIL   PERMIT NO. 717   BUFFALO, NY

POSTAGE WILL BE PAID BY ADDRESSEE

SILHOUETTE READER SERVICE
3010 WALDEN AVE
PO BOX 1867
BUFFALO NY 14240-9952

NO POSTAGE
NECESSARY
IF MAILED
IN THE
UNITED STATES

ALTERNATE MEANS OF ENTRY: Hand print your name and address on a 3 x 5 piece of plain paper and send to: Silhouette's Million Dollar Sweepstakes III, 3010 Walden Ave., P.O. Box 1867, Buffalo, NY 14269-1867. Limit: One entry per envelope.

mother. There'd been no sadness, just an eagerness to escape.

"I'm ready."

Sam swung around.

Buttoning up a second sweater, Erin winked. "She agreed."

"She agreed?" he parroted.

Head bent, she slipped an arm into her coat. "Of course."

He couldn't help smiling as he held her coat collar while she slid her other arm into the sleeve. "You look smug."

She angled her face up to him. "I am."

Softly he pressed his lips to hers. How easy it would be to drown in her taste.

"Sam," she managed to say huskily, quelling a sigh.

"A thank-you," he murmured, and kissed her again quickly before grabbing her hand and tugging her along out the door.

The windshield wipers labored to shove snow to the corners of the windows. His eyes narrowed, Sam focused on the road while they drove over a hill and past the first of many small villages, the buildings' rooftops frosted with snow.

"Did you call Dorothy?" Bending forward, Erin angled the far right car vent toward her.

Sam dared a glance away from the road. "I told her Kathryn would be right over for Sara. How did you get her to agree?"

"It wasn't difficult. She was thrilled for a whole day with Sara." On the other hand, she'd glowered at the idea of Erin spending more time with Sam. Erin decided against telling him that. She unzipped her parka and tugged off her gloves as the car became warm and cozy.

Though it was early afternoon, he switched on the headlights. Flakes of snow hurtled toward the beams. "Playing peacemaker," he teased.

"If I can," she said honestly. "Have you had lunch?"

"Lunch?" Stopping for food meant delaying a trip he'd hoped to complete in daylight. "You haven't eaten?"

"I forgot." She poked a finger in the direction of a fast-food restaurant. "There's one."

"No wonder you're so damn thin."

"I've been eating quite well since I came home." Came home, she mused. For the past ten years, she'd thought of New York as home, but she was away from her apartment more than she was there. She'd never gotten a cat or a dog because she worked sixty hours most weeks. The only plants she had were silk because she'd known that real ones would wilt and die from neglect.

Sam smothered a hint of annoyance that was meant more for the weather than her, and steered the car into the take-out lane. "What do you want?"

Her brows knitting, she perused the outside menu.

"Today," he suggested with a laugh in his voice as he realized she still weighed every decision overlong.

"Okay." She kept staring at the menu, debating between a hamburger and a chicken sandwich. "A cheeseburger, fries and—no." She heaved a sigh. "A salad," she corrected herself, thinking of the drudgery of a diet ahead of her if she didn't show some willpower soon. Rituals before bedtime with moisturizers, routines with hair conditioners and aerobic classes seemed a world away, but she couldn't afford to forget them.

Silent, they drove past colonial-style homes set behind a row of towering elms, then through a town where the few houses were little more than cottages.

Finished munching on the salad, she dropped the plastic container back in the bag. "Want some music?"

"There are a bunch of CDs under your seat."

"All highbrow?"

He slanted a grin at her. "No, there's some noisy stuff in there. And lots of country music."

Erin raised a surprised brow and remained silent, waiting for an explanation.

"My daughter loves it," he said, then laughed.

"Therefore, you do?"

"We compromise." His eyes on the road, he held out his hand for his coffee cup. "She endures a little Beethoven while she's coloring. And together we listen to Garth Brooks and Reba McEntire while we're riding."

Erin said nothing. Sam had always been kind and caring about others. She sorted through the CDs. "Is Randy Travis okay with you?"

"That's fine." An upbeat, hand-clapping rhythm drifted through the car. "That's one of Sara's favorites, too."

Slowing as they approached another hamlet, Sam cast a worried glance at the low-hanging clouds hiding the mountain peaks. He knew Erin anticipated information that would exonerate Rory. Sam only envisioned a treacherous drive home in a storm.

By the time they reached Concord, the sunlight had completely vanished behind a mantle of thick heavy clouds that looked ready to smother an imposing church steeple and the State House tower.

They spent five minutes in the state capitol learning they had to backtrack to a neighboring town to speak to the authorities who'd executed the raid at the auto-parts shop.

When they arrived at the police precinct, a beefy man with a bushy gray mustache was laughing robustly at the rubber dagger he'd just unwrapped.

"What's going on?" Erin murmured.

Shrugging, Sam asked the same question of a uniformed officer blocking the door of a room decorated with blue-and-white streamers and red balloons.

"It's the chief's retirement party." He attempted a steely-eyed glare that was ineffectual for someone who didn't look like he shaved yet.

"Great timing," Sam grumbled.

Patiently they waited while presents were opened and a whipped-cream cake was cut. Fifteen minutes passed before Sam was slapping every piece of identification he owned onto the chief's desk. "I told you I'm the lawyer for a suspect in Stony Creek."

Head bent, the chief examined Sam's business card and driver's license. Only a phone call to Stony

Creek's sheriff brought any cooperation. "Sheriff says he knows you."

Discreetly Erin rolled her eyes.

"So what do you want?"

"To talk to the owner of the parts shop that you raided."

"Can't talk to him." As a gray-haired woman handed the chief a plate with a slice of cake fit for the Jolly Green Giant, he lost the growl in his voice. "Thank you, June."

"Why can't I?" Sam asked in a patient, respectful tone that the tightness of his jaw belied.

"He's out on bail."

Mentally Sam did a quick count to ten. "Could you tell us what you learned?"

"Nothing."

"Nothing?" Erin echoed.

"You heard right." He leaned back to sit on the edge of his desk. "He never told who sold him the parts."

"Honor among thieves," Sam murmured.

"Guess you could call it that."

"Are there any other auto-parts stores in town?"

The bridge of the chief's nose bunched upward. "Why would you want to know that?" he asked between forkfuls of cake.

Sam tiptoed professionally. "I guess you already talked to any of the owners to learn if they were approached by someone, maybe a guy named Techner."

"Where'd you get that name?"

Sam explained Ron Kale's story.

The chief shifted a meaty shoulder. "First I heard about that."

"Is there another auto-parts shop?"

"Nope." He pushed away from the edge of his desk and patted his rotund stomach. "But there's a general store that sells parts."

Sam prodded. "Around here?"

"Edge of town before the highway." With his fork, he pointed in one direction while shifting a look over his shoulder at the clock on the wall. "But Harley's probably closed. Doesn't stay open a minute longer than he needs to."

Smothering some choice words, Sam ushered Erin toward the exit.

"We came for nothing," she said, unable to veil her disappointment.

"We're not done yet."

Silent, Erin bundled up but wasn't prepared for the icy air or how much the temperature had plummeted. Shaking, she plowed with Sam toward his car. "Oh, it's freezing."

Without missing a step, he tugged her scarf up higher around her neck. A gusting wind swirled snow around them, blinding their path to his car. With an arm around her shoulders, Sam drew her along with him, releasing her only to struggle with the car door.

Her cheeks burning, she pressed gloved hands to her face and hunched forward inside the car to get nearer to the car's heater.

The iciness lingered.

Neither of them talked. A touch discouraged, Erin flicked the radio to a station known for soft contemporary music, then, slanting the air vent down at her feet, she wiggled numb toes inside her boots.

With the darkening of the sky, lights flicked off in the few businesses on the street. A newscaster cut in with more road closings. All of them led back to Stony Creek. A car ahead of them fishtailed and skidded to avoid ramming into a stalled car.

Driving slower, Sam spotted a sign at the edge of town advertising food and negotiated the car between a row of trucks in the parking lot of the diner.

Erin cast a questioning look at him. "You want to eat?"

He motioned at the building across the street. "After we go there."

Snow blocked several letters on the sign for Harley's General Store. Remembering the trek to the car earlier, Erin gauged the distance to the building across the street.

Together, they struggled against wind and snow. A step ahead of her, Sam fought a gusting wind and laid his weight against the door to hold it open for her.

Erin scooted forward, but the building offered shelter from the wind only and not the cold.

Dressed in a ski cap and heavy winter parka, the man behind the counter stood with arms crossed. "If you need something, it's good you came now because I'm closing in another minute. Furnace went out."

"We only need a moment of your time," Sam told the owner. Anxious for Erin as well as himself to seek warmth elsewhere, he quickly explained.

"Naw, never had any guy like that come in here."

Erin felt a weariness pressing down on her.

The man rounded the counter to lock the door. "I heard that my brother-in-law had some guy come in boasting a good deal on parts."

Erin swung around, suddenly hopeful.

"Said some young guy came in with one of those 'too good to be true' deals."

Inwardly she tensed. Young. The man had been young. She realized she'd been hoping for other words, maybe, even something that would point a finger at Don Willis.

"Did your brother-in-law buy the parts?" Sam asked while digging leather gloves out of his pockets.

"Doubt it." He wandered with Sam to where Erin was standing near the door. "He's a pretty sharp old guy. He's a farmer, potatoes mostly. In the winter, he does some side jobs, too, like repairing engines. Think he always wanted to be a grease monkey. But there was the farm and he was the oldest, so it was his business to take over."

"What's his name?"

"Dwayne—Dwayne Mostley. Lives in the next town," he added and offered directions to his relative's farm.

"It's a lead," Erin said over the wail of the wind as they stepped outside.

Shaking against a chill, Sam curled a hand under her arm and propelled her toward the diner. "Let's talk about this inside the café."

They battled their way across the street, against snow rushing around them. In a more forgiving manner, the wind whipped at their backs, pushing them forward.

Chapter Eight

A bell jingled above the door. Quaint and small, the restaurant was decorated with yellow-and-blue tablecloths and blue café-style curtains. It was bustling with activity, its two waitresses rushing around to take orders from a roomful of customers obviously, like Sam and Erin, looking for shelter from the storm.

They settled at the only vacant table. The aromas of corn bread and baked beans and roast lamb filled the room. Looking around her, Erin shed her gloves and scarf but kept on her parka. A thin blond girl took their orders for ham dinners and coffee.

Sam considered what they'd learned. Whether eager or not to pursue their lone lead, he didn't dare venture in any direction except toward home. "We can't check out Harley's brother-in-law tonight."

Erin sipped the coffee just set before her, cupping the mug and letting the warmth seep into her hands. "He said a young man tried to sell the parts."

He wasn't deaf to the catch in her voice that punctuated her anxiety. "Hey, it isn't Rory," he insisted. Despite his effort to ease her concern, Sam's mind shifted to the prosecutor's case. A better description, one that exonerated Rory, would be a big help. "If Mostley doesn't give us anything to prove that then we'll look somewhere else."

Whether it was lip service or not, she clung to his encouragement. "Thank you."

"For what? For doing my job?"

Erin cracked a weak smile. "For believing in him."

Shrugging off his jacket, he could have told her gratitude wasn't what he wanted.

"I feel better just knowing that we won't give up."

It wasn't in his nature to give up, yet he had years ago. And look at what he'd lost. "Tomorrow or the next day, I'll come back here and talk to Mostley."

They'd both come back, but Erin didn't bother to argue with him. "Maybe he can identify the man. If it matches Ron Kale's identification of Techner, then they'll know Ron isn't lying. At least, Rory won't have that charge against him."

"Maybe," he said absently.

Erin waved a hand in front of his face to gain his attention. "Where are you? What aren't you saying? And why aren't you?" she asked, a little unnerved. Though tactful when necessary, he was always straightforward.

"I'm speculating."

"Well, speculate with me," she insisted.

He laughed at her impatience. "I keep wondering why Don Willis is claiming he saw Rory. Why is he lying about seeing Rory?"

Erin cocked a brow. "Because he's involved?"

"Or—"

"Or what?" she asked, growing annoyed at having to pull the words out of him.

"Do you know his son?"

Erin drew back as the waitress delivered their dinners. It looked delicious, but she was more interested in the direction of Sam's thoughts. "That scrawny little boy?"

"Bobby Willis isn't little anymore," he said between bites. "You've been away a long time, Erin." He scooped up a forkful of mashed potatoes. "He's sixteen or seventeen now. He worked at Ron's Garage. You know, sweeping up."

"You think he's involved?"

"I'm not big on coincidences. Don Willis identifies Rory. His son worked at Ron's. Seems to me there should be some connection."

Her face lit with the kind of smile he recalled staring at hundreds of times. "You'd have been a pretty good gumshoe," she commented, settling down to eat her dinner.

He chuckled. "I'm a pretty good lawyer."

"In Boston, you didn't have to do your own investigating, did you?"

Sam thought about the slew of associates, managers and partners he'd worked with. "No, I didn't. That's the one advantage I had there. I wouldn't have to run around in a blizzard looking for evidence to help my client." As far as he was concerned, the trade-off was worth it. Whatever he lost by being in Stony Creek, he gained more whenever he took Sara ice skating and tobogganing. He recalled a promise to teach her how to windsurf and water-ski in the summer. He remembered the way her eyes had lit with excitement when the town had gathered at the village square to light the enormous Christmas tree. Somewhere else, he might find all of that to offer her, but would he have the time to be with her? "Do you still ski?" he asked, recalling some fun times with her.

Erin looked up from the dark brew in her cup. "Not very often. The last time I went was..." She considered the years that had passed. "Was with my husband when we were first married."

He wanted to know more, yet he didn't. "Where did you go?"

"Lake Tahoe." She spoke without thinking. "We had a wonderful time. We'd only been married a few months. The honeymoon stage."

"It didn't last long?"

"No. He had his work. I had mine. We didn't see a lot of each other. We grew apart. Probably we should never have married, but I thought it would work out. I thought we had something worth saving."

Sam couldn't stop himself from asking. "So what happened?"

"He drank. At first, I didn't think too much about it. Eventually, it seemed he couldn't live without the alcohol."

"What about help for him?"

"He had no problem." She met his eyes with a sad look. "That's what he said." Yelled. How many times had he been furious with her whenever she'd suggested help? "He didn't think he had a problem. There was nothing I could do to make him see he was heading for trouble."

"So you left him?"

Erin caught her breath with a memory of the last night she'd seen him. "We both decided there was no hope for us." The light touch of Sam's cold knuckles on her cheek forced her to look back at him. Though she'd endured some of the worst days, months, of her life, she'd always maintained control. Yet now, with a simple touch from him, she felt herself teetering on the edge of it. She pulled back, managing a smile to elude the melancholy mood slipping over her.

Talk to me, he silently urged. But he knew what it was like to bury a secret. Each day it was kept, it became more difficult to share until it seemed so deep inside a person it couldn't be exhumed. From the radio in a corner, Lionel Ritchie's smooth voice filled the room. Sam pushed his plate away. "An old song."

She'd been listening to the soft, lilting music. It was a song they'd danced to in the high school gymnasium with streamers and balloons overhead.

Across the table, her eyes met his. He recalled a red velvet dress that had shown off her slim waist. "Dance with me," he urged, offering her his hand.

Erin laughed. "Dance?" He pulled her to her feet before she could resist. Customers stared, mostly men who looked tired and in need of shaves. One elderly couple sat in a booth on the other side of the room and smiled knowingly. "This isn't the kind of place we should—"

"Come on," he urged as she rooted her feet to the tiled floor near the booth.

"They probably think we're crazy."

He watched her gaze sweep the room. "We all are or we wouldn't be caught out on a day like this."

"We had a good reason," she insisted, reluctantly following him to a small space closer to the music.

Smiling, he gathered her in his arms as if she belonged there. He felt her heartbeat quicken, felt the length of her relaxing against him. "That's what they think, too."

She tilted her head so her lips were a hairbreadth from his. "But we're the ones who are dancing."

Her fragrance teased him, making him wonder where she'd dabbed it. "And they're jealous."

With a touch so light that she barely felt it, his mouth caressed her ear. "Are you trying to confuse me?" she asked huskily.

Why not? he mused. She'd done the same to him since that moment when he'd seen her at the police station.

Her pulse racing at an uneven pace, she thought a reminder might help both of them. "We failed at this once before."

Again he pressed his mouth to her cheek. "Know what?"

Silly question. She could barely think with the heat of him so near. How could she know anything? she wondered. To her, everything bordered on crazy. "What?"

"We didn't fail. We never tried," he murmured close to her ear. "This time we could win."

Nothing between them was simple. Didn't he realize that this time when they went their separate ways, and they would, she would have opened a wound so raw that it would scar for life?

"I want you," he whispered so softly he sent a shiver through her. "I always have."

Breathless, for an instant, she could barely meet the intensity of his stare. "Why are you saying this now?" At eighteen, she'd have treasured those words. "If that were true, why didn't you say something before?"

"Before, you wanted more than I could give you." With the back of his hand, he grazed her cheek with his knuckles. He'd told her he wouldn't pressure her, and he found himself doing just that. "Think about now. That's all I ask."

Behind him, an arctic blast rushed in with the opening of the door.

"Man, have you been out there?" A man stopped a foot inside the diner, talking to anyone who'd pay attention to him. Tiny icicles clung from the brim of his hat, snow coated his boots. Red-faced, he shivered. "It's godawful cold."

Reluctantly Sam dropped his hand from her waist and stepped back. "We'd better get going."

Overhearing him, the trucker guffawed. "You ain't gonna get your car started, man." Sam halted as he reached into the back pocket of his Levi's for his wallet as the trucker rambled over to their table. "Me and another trucker tried everything to get his rig started."

A tray of food in her hand, the older waitress offered a solution. "If you need a place to stay, the inn next door might have a room."

The trucker scratched his unshaven jaw. "Might do just that."

"Stay in," Sam said to Erin. Snow blew against the window, fogging anything from view that was more than a foot away. "I'll go out and see if I can start the car."

His collar raised, he whipped a knit cap from his pocket and slipped it on his head. In anticipation of the frigid weather, he protectively turned his shoulders in before opening the door. Howling louder, the wind seemed to be laughing at anyone who dared face it.

Through the blinding sheet of flakes, he saw cars buried to their tires and stuck in a haphazard fashion on the highway. He struggled through knee-high drifts and wrestled with the wind to open his car door. Behind the steering wheel, he shook as the rush of freezing air seeped in from any opening it could find.

It took only a second to know the trucker had made an accurate call. Paralyzed, the engine wouldn't crank.

Through a flurry of snow, Sam squinted at the remodeled farmhouse that had been converted into a country inn. For tonight, they were stuck there.

Muttering, his head bent, he fought his way back to the café. It wasn't going to be an easy or restful night.

Inside the inn, a short, plump woman with white curls stood amid five of the truckers. With her smile, her round cheeks puffed. "All of you were out on a night like this?"

Behind Sam, more people crowded in.

"Name's Mrs. Billsby. I bet you're all tired."

"Lady, I just want a place to be warm, grab a few winks," the one trucker said in a slow southwestern drawl.

Nodding understandingly, she looked past him to Erin. "Both of you are stranded, too? My goodness."

Erin ended her viewing of the sitting room, its walls decorated with a floral design, and smiled at the woman. "Do you have any rooms?"

"Hell, I don't care about a room," one of the men grumbled. "I'll flop on the stairs if you'll let me."

Sam eyed the telephone on a small cherrywood desk. "Is your phone working?" he asked, trying to make eye contact with the woman despite a brawny back blocking her view of him.

"Yes, it is."

"Can I use it? It's an in-state call," he assured her.

As she waved a hand in the direction of the telephone, Sam cupped a hand under Erin's arm and steered her toward it.

She balked enough to slow his stride. "A room. We need rooms."

"We need to call your mother."

A second passed before Erin registered what he was really saying. Her mother wasn't his concern; Sara was.

"You talk to her first," Sam insisted as she cooperated and ambled with him to the phone.

Erin, too, thought that was the wisest approach.

Unzipping his jacket, Sam leaned against the wall near the oversize fireplace while she dialed the phone number. It occurred to him that he'd have skied home if possible rather than miss putting Sara to bed. During the years since Jill's death, he'd never spent a night away from Sara, not once.

"Mom, it's Erin." She readied herself for dozens of maternal questions.

"Where are you? I've been so worried."

Erin recapped everything they'd learned regarding Rory, then gave their location. "We're stuck here. The roads are impassable."

A moment of quiet followed. Was her mother weighing her safety versus her being with Sam? "Do you think you'll be home by morning?"

"Oh, I sure hope so."

"I wouldn't want you on the road. It's so bad."

Erin sensed her thoughts had traveled back to Jill and the snowy, icy night when she'd died.

"Erin, you be careful."

"I will be," she assured her, but wasn't certain if the warning was meant for more than the blizzard. Erin glanced at Sam standing beside her. "Mom, Sam needs to talk to you."

"About what?"

"Sara."

"Tell him that she came home early. They closed school."

Sam didn't need to hear Kathryn's response to know that she'd refused. "Ask her—" He waited for Erin to cup a palm over the receiver. "I've never been away from Sara before like this." Concern slipped into his voice. "Ask Kathryn if she's there so I can talk to her."

"Mom, is Sara there?"

"No, she's next door visiting Timmy."

Erin shook her head. "At Timmy's."

Sam kneaded muscles tightening at the base of his neck. During serious talks with Sara, she'd questioned him about Jill. She'd revealed her worry that he could leave her like her mother had. Sam held out a hand. "Give me the phone."

She hesitated, not sure what her mother might do, including hanging up on him.

"Kathryn, it's Sam. Don't hang up," he insisted, obviously coming to the same conclusion that Erin had. "Kathryn, she's going to be troubled. Would you tell her I called? Please. Tell her—tell her I'll be home tomorrow. Tell her that I love her." He waited, counting seconds, wondering if she'd set down the receiver, if they'd been disconnected.

"I'll tell her what you've said."

He didn't realize he'd been holding his breath until that moment. "Thank you."

"May I speak to my daughter?"

It was easier to ignore the curtness in Kathryn's voice now that he had her reassurance. He gave the receiver back to Erin, then wandered to Mrs. Billsby.

"Where are you staying?" Kathryn questioned sharply, drawing Erin's attention back to her.

Erin stared at the pottery and gleaming copper utensils adorning the fireplace mantel and shelf. The blazing fire held captive several men and a young couple, like them, who'd been caught in the storm. "At an inn. It's very nice, and the woman who owns it seems to be taking in as many people as she can just to give them shelter."

"That's good." Kathryn sounded relieved to know a crowd surrounded them. "According to the television, the whole state is caught in an unexpected snowstorm. I wish you were home."

"I know." Erin wished she could reach through the phone and give her a reassuring hug. "But I'm all right. I need to go, Mom," she said, peripherally noticing a trucker shifting impatiently to use the phone. "You will tell Sara what Sam asked you to, won't you?"

"Erin, I may dislike the man intensely, but my granddaughter's welfare is important to me. I wouldn't want her upset. Now, you take care of yourself, and tell *him* to drive carefully when you do start for home."

Glancing her way, Sam noted the deep breath Erin took as she set the receiver back in its cradle. One difficult moment was following the next, he mused. "We've got a problem."

Erin looked at Mrs. Billsby, rather than him.

"I have one room left," she announced.

Talk about complications. Erin imagined a bunch of them if she and Sam occupied the same room.

Sam noted the line of indecision furrowing her brow. It would have been easy to worm his way into that room with her. But he couldn't pressure her. Call it an underlying romantic streak, but it wasn't the way he wanted her. "Do you snore?"

She looked affronted. "Of course not."

He sent Mrs. Billsby a dubious look. "Women always say that."

The woman's face turned rounder with her smile. "Such a tease."

"She'll take it," he told the woman.

Erin felt forced to ask. "Where will you sleep?"

He delivered his best boyish grin to the inn's owner. "Would it be all right if I camped out in your sitting room?"

"On a night like this, do you think I'd turn you away? Of course you can, but you'll have a roommate or two."

Truckers from the café were already claiming nesting rights. One draped himself across an antique-looking sofa while another one slouched in a corner chair. A too-short settee and the floor were the only available spaces left. "Can I get a blanket?"

"Plenty of them," the woman assured him. She placed a wrinkled hand on Erin's shoulder. "If you wait a minute, I'll give you the key to your room."

Climbing the stairs, Erin looked back over her shoulder. Bent forward, Sam was testing the cushions of a short, flowered settee. Two of his roommates had already crashed and sounded like chain saws.

Halfway up, she sighed. No reasoning, no sensibility, would help her dodge guilt. She'd get no rest, feeling lousy about taking the only available room. "Sam."

Turning, he looked toward the stairs. Shadowed, a light from a hallway lamp on the second floor radiating across her face, she looked so beautiful that he ached.

"This is crazy," she said softly. "Come on. You won't get any sleep here."

He wished like hell his heart wasn't pounding as if he'd been racing a marathon. With a blanket and pillow caught in his arm, he wound his way around furniture to reach the stairs. "Feel sorry for me?"

"You need sanctuary from the nasal kings of the world." A hand on the banister, she swiveled a look over her shoulder. "But I get the bed."

"It's a long way to the top of these stairs," he murmured, following her. "You might change your mind."

Erin reached the top and faced him. They stood eye-to-eye. She tried to ignore the tensing of her body, the lightning-quick thrill skittering through her as he fingered strands of her hair.

Unsteady, she held on to the banister and scrambled for control. What had she been thinking? What was it she really wanted? Not to be lovers. She'd been feeling sorry for him, imagining him cramped on that settee that was a foot too short for him. She hadn't asked him for any other reason, she tried to convince herself.

Staring into eyes filled with uncertainty, he wanted to hold her until she admitted what he'd already realized. They should have been together years ago. For a second, he inhaled deeply to absorb her scent. He taunted himself, wanting to bury his face in the silky strands of her hair. Instead, he let them slip through his fingers and gave her space.

"We were lucky to get the last room," she murmured, laboring to concentrate on something else, anything but him and the desire rising inside her. With a turn, she stepped away, concerned now she might not manage a minute more with him without weakening.

Watching the easy sway of her hips, Sam mentally moaned. "Yeah, real lucky."

They stood at the doorway to the room. All she saw was the bed and one chair.

Under his breath, Sam murmured a few choice words. As she scurried forward, he dumped his pillow and blanket to the floor.

Expecting him to be sprawling in the chair, Erin stopped at the side of the bed. "You're going to sleep there?"

"The way I see it, it's here or the bathtub unless you've changed your mind about—"

"The tub would probably be too short."

He'd never force the moment. He wanted her to be as desperate, as needy, as caught up in the heat, as he was. "That's sort of what I thought."

Her back to him, she heard the rasping sound of his zipper. "Hard floors are good for the back."

Sam told himself to be satisfied with a warm, quiet room. He eased down to the hooked rug and imagined a soft mattress. "Oh, yeah, this is a nice hard floor."

Erin smiled to herself.

"And flat, too."

She couldn't help it. She giggled.

"I heard that."

She turned the knob on the lamp to darken the room.

The nonchalance cost him. "You know what?"

She frowned. "What?"

"They clean under the beds."

In the darkness, she could see the flash of his smile.

Quickly she slipped out of her jeans. Snuggling under a down comforter and a fringed chenille bedspread, she struggled not to think how close he was. She visualized warm summer days, the Queen Anne's lace that bordered the ocean's shoreline near the coastal towns, the peaks of the mountains white beneath a summer's sunlight. The pleasant images didn't help. Complicated emotions and confused thoughts had her staring at the dark ceiling again and thinking.

Since her daughter's death, she wasn't sure she'd have managed her career or anything else if she hadn't put emotions on a back burner. Months after her divorce, after her child's death, had been a living hell. She'd always thought the phrase a cliché. She knew better now.

There was so much risk in reaching out to Sara, even more to Sam. It had been a long time since she'd thought of herself as a woman needing anyone, but needs were alive inside her. She desperately wanted what had never been. She wanted a memory to treasure when she left.

For the umpteenth time since Sam had curled up and burrowed under the blanket, he rolled over. Burying his head beneath the pillow proved futile. Out of sorts, he punched the pillow, settled his head down, and stared out the window, trying to ignore the faint scent of woman so near. Snowflakes fell furiously. A slice of moonlight streaked across the dark icy stillness of night. He stared for a long time, content to listen to the sound of her soft breathing, then eased up on an elbow to look at her. Pale beneath the shadow of night, she looked beautiful, fragile in the silver light piercing into the room, streaking across her dark hair. As she shifted on the mattress, he could visualize long, lean limbs, the curve of her waist, the paleness of her skin.

"Sam."

If he hadn't known better, he'd have thought he was dreaming, imagining the sound of her voice. "Yeah."

"I feel guilty."

He gave a short laugh and stared at the dark ceiling. "Good."

"Really guilty."

The softness in her voice swirled around him like a caress. He propped his elbow on the floor again and stared up at her. As a slender pale hand stretched out to him, his gut clenched. He'd been waiting for this moment with her for a long time. Silent, uneasy that even a word would snatch away what seemed like a dream, he pushed to a stand. Resisting a moan at the ache in his back, he wandered to the bed.

Desire pounded through him when invitingly, she held up the blanket for him. Still, he moved slowly. When he sank to the mattress, his mind wasn't on its softness. Despite the distance between them, he could feel the heat of her body. His face inches from hers, he searched her eyes, darkening to the color of a blue deep enough to drown in, eyes filled with desire, seduction.

She knew she'd be baring more than her body to him. Vulnerable, as if under a spell, she inched closer. Even as she braced herself for sensation, nerves jumped when his leg brushed hers. Darkness mantled his face, but she saw his slow grin. Need hummed through her. Reaching out, she grazed his rib cage with her fingertips.

A fire burning within him, he caught the nape of her neck with his hand. "I never thanked you for rescuing me."

"No, you didn't," she whispered. Concerns fled beneath a mightier force. Close to him, she took a shallow breath. He felt wonderful. Warm. Strong. If there were no demands, if she made love with him but didn't fall in love, she'd keep her heart safe, she reasoned while she still could.

Lightly he touched the sharp point of her hip, the side of her thigh. Their breaths mingled, their mouths nearly met. She wouldn't listen to her head anymore. Invitingly she parted her lips beneath the gentle pressure of his. It felt so good, so right to be with him.

With her against him, with every breath he drew, her scent intoxicated him a little more. He knew he wasn't any less vulnerable than she was. Even as clawing need rushed over him, he warred with it. "You know what I want," he said on a harsh breath.

"What I want," she murmured against his mouth. A heady sensation passed over her. She vowed she wouldn't expect too much. Few things in life were lasting, but she'd played a game of pretenses too long, pretending she felt only friendship for him, pretending she hadn't hurt when he'd married Jill, pretending she wasn't longing for him. "Make love with me," she whispered.

He wanted to close his eyes, absorb the moment, the feel of her breasts pressing against his chest, the heat of her breath caressing his face. His heart hammering, he held back for another second. "Be sure," he said softly, his mouth hovering near hers.

Yearning, she slid an arm around his bare back. "I've never been more sure. I've always wanted you," she murmured before her lips met his.

His mouth possessed with a promise, with persuasion, with aching pleasure. The chill of the night danced across her skin, but she was warm, matching the hunger of the lips moving over hers and the tongue tempting and exploring the warmth of her mouth. To be wanted was part of the joy of loving. She'd missed that and the pleasure of sharing. But she hadn't wanted just any man.

As he filled himself, his mouth tasting as if he'd starved for this moment, she clung, plunging herself deeper into the abyss of feelings she'd stifled for months. Her mind reeled, focusing on the soft touch of his hand roaming over her. As if she had no will of her own, she followed the command of his hands, lifting her arms to shed her sweatshirt.

With a pride-stripping desperation, she tugged at his T-shirt, wild to mold herself to him. There were no barriers. They stripped them away with the same rush of need that cloth was shed. Like a butterfly's caress, his lips trailed down her neck across flesh bathed by a silvery sheen.

Sam touched what he'd imagined. Urged on by the arching of her body as if to draw them closer, he let his tongue roll over velvety soft flesh. He meant to go slow, but she moved beneath him in a sensuous slow motion. It lit the fire. Driven by the sound of her sighs, her quickened breaths, he lowered his head to take her with him.

The past didn't matter, couldn't at that moment. She was coming alive again because of him. Where he caressed, she tingled. Where he kissed, she warmed. Over and over again, he aroused her with a brush of his fingers or the moistness of his tongue. Lost in the moment, she stroked flesh hot with passion, then shifted and let her mouth caress the tense ripples across his stomach, the warmth of a thigh. Like she'd never done before, she gave to him.

Pleasure and power whipped through him. Years of wanting tumbled together and merged. He murmured her name as she took him into her body. Eyes met and held before he pressed down on her, before flesh fused. Then bodies moved with a oneness he'd thought impossible.

He imagined there might be only once in a lifetime that a man would or could feel like this. It was with him again. The quick passion, the throbbing, the yearning he'd thought he'd left behind in his youth. And something more, something deep and stirring inside him.

With her tight to him, giving him all of her warmth and softness, he closed his eyes against the darkness.

Sunlight and morning meant thinking about tomorrows. For now, he only wanted to remember tonight.

Gentle hands, caressing kisses, passion swirling her into a mindless fantasy. All of it was with her again when sunlight peeked through the lace curtains. Waking with a lover was something she'd given up. She'd never expected to feel desire like this again. Perhaps she'd never known it.

The sound of rushing water tugged her from the last vestiges of sleep. Pushing back her hair, she turned her face toward the faint heat of the sun. Only light flurries swayed with the wind. Across the room, their boots mingled, the toe of his left boot propped against the heel of hers, his T-shirt tossed on top of her sweatshirt.

She lay still, simply absorbing the lingering scent of him, listening to the running water. When it stopped, she considered how to handle the next few minutes. She'd invited him, wanted him, but she didn't want more than—what? His body? God, but that sounded awful, and it wasn't even true. She yearned just as much for his laughter and his companionship. So it wasn't a matter of what she wanted. It narrowed down to what she didn't want—pressure, demands, soft words of love.

Bare to the waist, Sam sauntered out of the bathroom with a towel in his hand. Standing beneath the water, he'd wondered about these first moments in the light of day. If there had been no snowstorm, no forced night together, would she have ever reached out to him?

Snuggling beneath the blanket, she watched him. Moisture shone on his fair hair and across his shoulders. When he reached for his shirt, she admired flesh she'd touched and tasted. "Morning."

The soft sleepy sound whipped him around. He caught the sweep of her gaze over him and felt a nudge of pleasure. "I thought you were still sleeping."

Fascinated by the ripple of muscles at his stomach, she returned a sleepy smile. "Why did you get up?"

"You took all the blankets," he said to keep the moment light.

"I did not." Erin viewed the jumbled sheets and blanket wrapped tightly around her legs. His boyish, cocky grin made her laugh. "You're impossible. You still tease unmercifully." With his long, quiet look, a slow-moving heat moved over her. So did morning-after nerves. To avoid his stare, she turned her head toward the window. "It's almost stopped snowing."

"Too bad." Sam closed the distance to her and settled on the edge of the mattress. "Do you have a problem?"

She made herself look at him. "Last night—"

Because the hint of doubt in her eyes was arousing his own uncertainty, he placed a finger to her lips to silence her. "Don't tell me you regret it."

How could she when she was aching again for him? "I love snowstorms now."

A cloud of worry hovered over him. Taking her hand, he kissed her palm. "But?"

"No, there isn't one," she assured him. "Here or at home, I'd have admitted the truth."

A palm on each side of her, he bent closer. "What's that?"

She felt his smile against her throat. "I wanted you."

Those words enticed him as much as the soft flesh at her collarbone.

"But—"

Frowning, Sam lifted his head. "I knew there was one."

The need to touch overwhelmed her. She brushed his cheek. "But I don't expect more, Sam."

He knew that but didn't understand anything except she'd been hurt. For now, he'd play it her way. "Okay," he answered, because to say more might make her run. "Move over." He tugged off his towel and edged in beside her.

She saw no logic in what was happening between them. More kisses, more moments such as this would lead nowhere. But as simple as that sounded, she couldn't deny that she wanted him. Hot and quick sensations sprinted through her as his mouth grazed her flesh. She snuggled closer, everything she believed drifting further away. "Did you sleep well?"

"So-so." His voice softened to a caressing whisper.

With a sigh, she closed her eyes in response to his fingers playing across her thigh. "What was wrong?"

"You snore," he murmured against the round curve of her breast.

"I—"

"Softly," he added before lowering his head.

Chapter Nine

The inn's dining room beckoned with its beamed ceiling, spindle-back chairs and crackling fireplace. Mrs. Billsby's culinary talent nearly had her last-minute guests drooling at the buffet table.

Her plate loaded with scrambled eggs and bacon and wonderful-looking blueberry muffins, Erin settled on a chair at the table beside Sam and listened to the trucker across from them.

Enthusiastically he shoveled eggs into his mouth. "I wonder if this town owns a snowplow," he said, showing an eagerness to continue his run to Virginia.

One of Mrs. Billsby's helpers, a young teenage girl, supplied an answer, "Harley—he owns the general store."

"We've met him," Erin said, reaching for a second muffin.

"He'll run the snowplow through. When he feels like it," Mrs. Billsby piped in. "This afternoon, sometime probably."

Groans mingled with a few indecipherable whispered oaths.

"What about someone who can give me a jump start?" Sam asked between bites.

"That would probably be Harley, too."

Sam elbowed Erin and spoke low, "Our lives belong to Harley."

She let out a little breath to stifle a giggle.

They ate, listening to the truckers' tall tales about other storms.

Finished with breakfast, Erin cradled her cup in her hands. Beside her, Sam stared out the window, appearing lost in his own thoughts. She didn't need psychic power to guess what was bothering him. "Are you thinking about Sara?"

A wry smile curved his lips. "I'm wondering..." He held back any criticism of Kathryn. "She's probably loving this storm. She's crazy about making snowmen."

Erin placed her hand over his. "She's okay."

"I'm sure she is. Kathryn will take good care of her."

"Sam, she gave me her word that she would tell Sara you called and what you said."

He sort of laughed at himself. "I know it's nuts, but we've never been apart before."

Erin couldn't have imagined him ever saying something so sweet. "And you miss her?"

"I worry. She—she knows people can be taken from her. She's talked about not having a mommy, and..." With amazing clarity, he remembered the night Sara had crawled on his lap after a bad dream and clung to him and pleaded with him never to leave her. "I've tried to reassure her about me."

"I think it's natural that she'd be a little scared. You're everything to her." She knew how frightening it was to lose the person you loved the most.

. Done with breakfast, they ventured outside. Folds of snow shrouded the ground, burdened tree branches and buried cars.

Moving a few steps ahead of him, she stilled and swiveled a look back. His head turned away, he was frowning at the drifts of snow, at the impassable street.

"Aha, hear it? It sounds like Harley and his trusty snowplow are—" As a snowball whizzed past his head, he whipped around. "Hey!"

Laughing, she was bending down and packing more snow between her gloves.

"You're in trouble, Delaney," he called out in a feigned threatening tone.

With his movement closer, she danced an awkward step backward, then wisely tossed aside the snow she was packing in her gloves, guessing retreat was safer than fighting. She ran, sort of. Ten steps of lifting her legs through the knee-high snow and she collapsed.

Sam fell down beside her and rolled her on top of him. "What did you call that?"

Humor danced in her eyes. "A sneak attack."

A hand at the back of her neck, he held her still. "So's this," he advised, smothering her laughter with a kiss. He'd made a mistake years ago. He'd let the right woman go, the one who would complete his life, who would bring the sunshine in even on the coldest and dreariest New Hampshire days. And now he didn't know if it was too late. But he had to try. Dammit, he had to try.

Breathless, she didn't move. He made her question everything. He made her world tilt. He made her feel like the young girl who'd left years ago—the one who'd been in love with him.

Accepting his hand, she swayed against him when he drew her to her feet. For a long moment, she stayed in his arms. It would be so easy to accept everything she'd denied for so long. Too difficult, too. A storm had brought them closer together. For a while, the world had narrowed, and it had been just the two of them. But there were others to be concerned with.

"You're thinking too much," he teased, placing a gloved finger to the faint frown line between her brows.

Didn't he see the complications?

"Why don't we just see what happens this time?" He stroked her cheek. "That's the way you want it, isn't it?"

"Yes."

"Then let's call it what it is." Watching her frown deepen, he smiled. "I love being with you. I always have."

But it wasn't that simple. What about her mother who'd feel betrayed if she got too close to him? She nearly laughed at her own thought. How much closer could she get? She'd known her mother's feelings about him, hadn't doubted her, yet she'd never questioned him about the night Jill had died.

Instead, she'd befriended him while enduring her mother's inflammatory remarks. Why? The answer came effortlessly. Because she believed in him. She knew his gentleness, knew no matter what her mother said about him, that he couldn't have done anything wrong. Despite all the years apart, she'd reacted instinctively to him with blind faith.

"Hey." He laughed easily. "Why are you still frowning?"

"We're not kids anymore, Sam. I can't ignore the feelings of other people."

A dull overbearing heaviness slipped over him. "You mean your mother?"

"Yes. I'm too old to sneak out to be with you." She rubbed snow from her gloves. "Here, alone with you, I could forget everything else. But we'll go back. It'll be difficult to be together." She measured her next words carefully. "All the time we've been together, you've never talked about the night Jill died. Never told me what happened."

She saw indecision in his face as if he were engaged in a private battle. "Tell me," she pleaded. "Don't you realize how torn I am? She was my sister. I need to know.''

His voice was calm and quiet. "And if I hurt her?"

Their gazes clashed.

"Did you?" She tried to catch her breath. Oh, God, she didn't want to hear this. Yet, she had to hear it.

"What if I did?" With a turn of his shoulder, he made her feel as if they were strangers. "Then is everything between us wrong?"

How could it be? she wondered. This was the man who'd caressed her, who'd made lost dreams seem a breath away. Her lover. Her friend. A gentle man. A loving one to her, to a small child. "You didn't hurt her," she returned, instinctively knowing she was right.

Tension eased from his face. "No, I didn't," he said so softly it was barely audible. "She left because she wanted to. She told me she wanted out of the marriage." He didn't face her. "That's it."

Erin stared at him. His back remained too rigid. What wasn't he telling her? Why wasn't he? "So she just left even though it was storming outside?"

Sunlight blasted at his eyes. Narrowing his gaze, he watched the progress of the snowplow. Feeling trapped more by his integrity with her than her persistence, he snapped words at her. "I don't know what she was thinking."

Aware emotion was rising in both of them, Erin waited a long second. "And was she leaving Sara with you?" she asked.

That whipped him around. He thought she knew him better. "Do you think I'd let her take our baby out in that storm?"

Shaking her head, she depended on reasoning. Her sister had left without Sara, if what he said was true. If it had been her, she wouldn't have left her daughter. She'd have waited, stayed with him until morning rather than leave her child. Something still didn't make sense.

Sam made a mistake. He met her stare. He'd expected accusations. He could have dealt with them. What he saw were questions, a need to understand. "Oh, God, Erin, let it go."

Because a tinge of a plea edged his voice, she knew she couldn't. "Tell me," she said softly, stepping closer.

"Why?"

No anger marked his voice. All she saw was regret. Framing his face with her hands, she begged, "Please. Why did she leave?"

Nearby, Harley and his snowplow shoved snow from the street. Why couldn't he push the past away as easily? he wondered. "She was meeting someone."

It took a moment to let his words sink in. "She was having an affair?"

A sad, ironic smile curved his lips. "Someone who'd vacationed near Stony Creek. The mayor's nephew," he finally said, even forcing out the man's name. "She'd met him when we'd come to visit your mother. He smooth-talked her, I guess. They kept in touch, were seeing each other, sometimes in Boston. That night she was meeting him."

Not fair, she thought, imagining how much her sister had brought back painful memories of his mother. "Sam—" Erin stopped herself from drawing him closer as her mother's harsh words returned. "No." She shook her head. "You're still lying to me."

The look of disbelief in her eyes rocked him. Everything they'd gained hung in the balance of his next words.

It took effort to speak with calm. Erin measured her words slowly. "You said you wouldn't let her take the baby. But my mother said you told her you weren't home. That you'd left Jill alone, and when you came back she was gone."

Sometimes saying anything was too much. Hadn't he watched enough criminals trip themselves in lies to know better? "She was walking down the steps when I came home, the suitcase in her hand. That's when she told me that she was leaving, she told me who she was meeting, about everything."

What he purposefully hadn't said buckled her knees. Erin touched his shoulder. "Without the baby? She was leaving the baby alone?"

Cold, flat eyes met hers. "What can I say? If I lie, you keep pushing. You want the truth so damn bad. Yes," he said angrily. "She didn't care enough to stay. She left the baby alone. She was on her way to meet her lover and that's all she cared about."

Chilled suddenly, Erin pulled her scarf higher on her neck. "Oh, God, Sam." How could her sister have done that?

"I'm sorry."

Erin forced her head up. "Sorry? For what?"

"That you made me tell."

All she could think about was all this time her mother had believed he was the one who'd done something wrong. "Why didn't you tell my mother about the affair?"

Looking up at the gray sky, he let the crisp wind whip at his face. "She was grieving enough, Erin. She didn't need to hear that."

Aching for him, she ran her fingers in a caress over the hair at the nape of his neck. "Sam, it's not fair to you. My mother blames you. If you told her the truth—"

"I can't do that to her."

No words of love could have touched her more deeply.

"Erin, years ago, Kathryn was special to me. My mother was gone. My father never—never talked to me. He set down rules, he insisted on certain things being done, but we never talked. I had no one. Then I started dating you, and Kathryn came into my life. She was everything I hadn't had since I was ten, everything that my own parent wasn't. No." He shook his head. "I won't hurt her. I can't."

To argue with him seemed futile. She shifted closer to him to comfort, to feel the same oneness as the night before.

With her weight against him, he had one thought, one wish—that nothing would separate them this time. But would fate be so generous? As much as she'd become a part of his and Sara's lives, she no longer belonged in the world he'd chosen for them. Could he change her mind? It was a question he couldn't answer. All he knew was that for now, for a while, she was his.

Together, they wandered up the inn steps, reaching it as the door swung open.

"Looks like we're out of here, folks," the brawny trucker announced. "Snowplow's cleared the highway. If you want, I'll give you a hand with your car. Figured you're anxious to leave, too."

Daylight had faded by the time Sam pulled into Kathryn's driveway.

"Do you want me to go in alone for Sara?" Erin asked.

It was an easy way out. Sam hadn't taken that route since Jill had died. "No, I'll go with you." Beneath the light in the car, he checked his wristwatch. It was past Sara's bedtime. He hoped that she was asleep. Little as she was, she amazed him with her ability to sense moods in others, especially anger. He'd like to avoid her witnessing Kathryn's toward him.

Erin entered the house ahead of him to find her mother engrossed in a new crime dram on television.

With the click of the door, Kathryn's head snapped in her direction. "Thank goodness you're home. I thought you wouldn't be back before another storm began." Her gaze slid to Sam standing in the doorway. She gave him a funny look. The one she turned on Erin was charged with motherly accusations.

Erin had known her mother would sense something had changed. Though she and Sam weren't touching or looking at each other, her mother's radar was working. "Is Sara sleeping?"

"Yes," she said stiffly. "She's in your room."

No welcome mat in front of him, Sam plunged forward. "I'll get her, then."

Grim-faced and tight-lipped, Kathryn snagged Erin's arm before she could pass her to follow him. "Erin, whatever's happened, stop now. Stay away from him."

"What if I said I can't?" she responded honestly.

Impatience snapped in her mother's eyes. "You never stopped caring for him, did you?"

A need to defend him flooded in on her.

"He isn't the person you remember."

No, he was more gentle, more patient, and he was being treated terribly.

"He already hurt one of my daughters. Must I watch him hurt another?"

"He won't," Erin said assuringly.

The sound of footsteps whirled them both around.

With Sara in his arms, Sam crossed the room to the door. Tension rippled in the air. A look at Erin's eyes announced a message he'd expected. He didn't need to overhear the conversation between mother and daughter to guess he'd been the one discussed. "Thank you, Kathryn," he said softly, not to wake Sara.

Anger reddened her cheeks. She whipped away, mumbling, "I'm her grandmother. Does he think he has to thank her grandmother for watching her?"

Draping a small afghan around Sara, Erin turned a sympathetic look on him. If he hadn't thanked her mother, she'd still have criticized him. "You can't win."

He stilled at the doorway. More important to him, could they?

"Daddy?" Sara opened her eyes to sleepy slits.

Cuddling her closer, he kissed her forehead. "It's okay. We're going home."

I wish we were alone again, Erin thought. I wish there was another snowstorm and one more night alone. Just the two of us. Lovingly she stroked the top of Sara's head. No, there couldn't be just the two of them. Because she needed reassurance she was about to do the right thing, she leaned into his arm and sought a kiss. "Tomorrow's a big day," she said, reminding him about the birthday party. "I'll be over early."

Bringing her to his side, he kissed her temple. He wanted more time, needed to know that everything gained wouldn't slip away again. He understood intense wanting. It only grazed the surface of his need for her. "Come with me now."

How easy it would be to say yes, she realized, but she couldn't. Placing a hand on his back, she affectionately nudged him forward. "Sara's expecting a big bash tomorrow. Remember?"

"A big bash," he murmured and narrowed his eyes as if trying to see into the future. "How much damage can twelve little kids do?"

"You'll find out."

The moment she closed the door, she considered the difficult moments ahead of her. Whatever intentions she had faded within seconds with the realization that her mother had gone to bed. Tomorrow. Early tomorrow, they'd talk, she decided while climbing the stairs.

Upon awakening, Erin gave herself no time to chicken out and marched toward the kitchen. At the table, Rory remained frozen like a statue with his nose buried behind the newspaper. "Where's Mom?"

He peeked over the top of the sports page. "Laundry room, I think."

Butterflies fluttered in her stomach. She thought of pouring herself a cup of coffee first, then resisted stalling.

The smell of fabric softener, sweet and clean, enveloped the small room off the back porch. Erin strolled up to the long table where her mother was folding clothes, and picked up a towel.

"After we last talked, did you learn any more that would help Rory?" Stiff and crisp, her mother's voice bore disapproval.

"No."

As Erin reached for a towel, her mother sent her a questioning look. "Have you suddenly had a yearning to do laundry?"

"I thought you could use help."

Her mother's features softened with a smile. "Thank you. But why don't you tell me why you're really here?" She slipped the towel from Erin's hands. "You always did this, you know."

Erin slanted a look at her. "Did what?"

"Cozied up to me and helped whenever you wanted something. Like that red velvet dress." A tinge of amusement lightened her tone. "You spent five nights in a row drying dishes and followed me for a week straight with your own dust rag. Never had such clean furniture. And all the time you were working up the courage to ask me about that dress that you'd seen on the rack at Louise's Boutique.''

''It cost a lot.''

''You looked lovely in it. But...'' Kathryn rolled a hand in front of her. ''Why don't you say whatever it is that you want to say?''

''It's Sara's birthday today.''

''Yes, I know.'' Kathryn reached into the basket for a T-shirt. ''All of five. Amazing how quickly they grow.''

''There'll be a big party for her.'' Without comment, her mother continued to fold the shirt. ''It's a special day for her.'' Erin forged ahead. ''And you'll miss it if you stay home.''

''I'll see her. I planned to go to the school, spend some time with her, give her her present.''

''It's not what she wants. She told me that she wants you at the party.''

Her mother's hands stilled. ''You know that's impossible.''

''It doesn't have to be.''

''I thought we already discussed him.''

Frustration churned inside her. If she could avoid revealing everything, she would. But she wasn't leaving until her mother agreed. ''For Sara, couldn't you go, couldn't you forget how upset you are with him?''

''No.'' Anger suddenly darkened her mother's eyes. ''And I don't know how you can go on...'' Her voice trembled. ''Go on seeing him when you know that he's never told me the truth about that night. For Jill's sake, no—I can't go. I won't pretend with him."

Erin gauged what words to say. "You know he cares a lot about you."

Slipping around her, Kathryn cut her off with a sharp response. "Erin, I don't want to discuss this."

"We have to." She backed up, blocking her mother's path to the door. "Mom, he does care about you. He always has. And it's because he does that he hasn't—"

Her mother's hand went to her arm. "Would you move, please?"

"Mom, he's been trying to protect you."

"Protect me?"

Her mother's combativeness gave way to puzzlement. Relieved, Erin leaned back against the table. "He knew how much you were grieving and . . ." She searched for words that wouldn't hurt her mother too much. Nothing would work but total truth, she realized. "Mom, she was leaving because there was another man."

"No." Kathryn shook her head. "See, you believe everything he says to you. He's lying. What man?" she demanded.

Erin spoke the name softly. "Do you remember him?"

"Of course I do," she said, staring at the tiled floor as if the man's face were drawn there. "She did like him. When she and Sam visited here, she saw him often, but she was simply being friendly."

"More than friendly." As her mother turned away, Erin persisted. "It's the truth. He was the man Jill left that night to meet."

Her back rigid, her mother shook her head. "You should believe in your sister."

"I can't." Erin saw no point in pretending. "She did a lot of things and didn't worry if they were wrong or not, or if she hurt someone."

"Oh, Erin. I remember, too, how you'd complain about her taking your sweater or lipstick, but that was one sister borrowing from another."

Erin shook her head. "That's not what I'm talking about. Mom, she lied to me. After I left town, I called home. She told me that she was dating Sam."

Her mother's head snapped up. "That's not true. They weren't dating. They didn't start dating until Christmas."

"Sam told me the same thing. But Jill lied to me. I'm sorry, but she did, and I walked away from someone I cared a great deal for—because of her."

Confusion deepened her mother's frown.

"Think about everything," Erin insisted. "It was Jill and not Sam who was unfaithful. How can you keep blaming Sam? And for what? He'd planned to come back here and hadn't for Jill's sake. She had the life she wanted, didn't she? Yet, she was spending time with another man."

"I know she saw a lot of..." She paused, seeming unable even to say the man's name.

"You know I'm right, don't you?"

"No!"

Erin couldn't avoid telling her more. "If Sam's guilty of anything, it's that he didn't tell you everything that happened because he cares so much about you."

"So he did lie."

"For your sake," Erin said softly. "Jill wasn't gone when Sam came home. She was leaving, and Sara wasn't with her. She was walking out without Sara."

"Without..." Reaching back, Kathryn slumped down on the chair against a wall. "Oh, God."

Erin ached at the pain in her mother's eyes.

For a long moment, Kathryn simply sat with her head bowed. "I don't want to believe any of this." She squeezed her eyes for a long moment. "And yet..." She paused and shook her head slowly. "One time Jill told me that she didn't want to be pregnant. I thought after Sara came, she'd feel differently, but I think she felt trapped by motherhood."

Erin sensed her mother wasn't making excuses for Jill's actions. She was trying to understand them.

"The last time when she and Sam were visiting me, I sensed their marriage wasn't going well. I asked why." She looked at Erin now. "Jill avoided answering me. Finally I asked her why she'd married Sam."

"Did she say that she married him because she loved him?"

Her mother was slow to respond. "No."

Erin wanted to ease her mother's mind. "I'm sure she did for a little while."

Sadness slipped into Kathryn's voice. "She wanted him because you had him. I suppose I always sensed that, but I never allowed myself to face the truth. I worried a lot about her. I used to wonder if your sister was ever really satisfied with what she had. I guess that's my fault. I spoiled her, but she seemed to need more than you or Rory," she added as an explanation. "So if she wanted something, I gave it to her. I was so grateful just to have her because she'd been sick when younger." Her voice trembled a little. "I'm sorry she hurt you, Erin," she said with anguish. "I'm really sorry."

Erin wished for soothing words. "None of that matters now." Cupping her mother's hands between hers, she said softly, "All that's important is Sara."

"The cake is here," Dorothy yelled out from the kitchen. She popped into the doorway leading to the living room and laughed at Sam. On the rug, he sat in the middle of a circle of balloons.

He held one out to her. "Here, blow up a balloon."

"Not me. We split duties. Mine included getting the cake, the ice cream, the plates, the hats and everything else," she said drawing out her last two words. "All you had to do was blow up a few balloons."

Sam held up the four bags of balloons. "A few?"

"What's all this yelling?" Erin asked from behind Dorothy. She peered over Dorothy's shoulder and smiled at the red, pink and purple balloons dancing in the air. "Need some help?"

"Blow up a balloon."

"I thought all lawyers were long-winded."

Cackling at his feigned scowl, Dorothy turned sideways to let her pass by.

Erin touched her hand. "Where's Sara?"

"Tammy's mother is picking her up from school."

"And taking her home with her so we have enough time," Sam added with an exaggerated wink as Dorothy disappeared back into the kitchen.

"What else has to be done?" Erin asked.

A devilish grin curved his lips. "Whatever."

Erin gave her head a little shake.

"You don't want to?" He pushed to a stand, intent on using a little persuasion to change her mind. Any notion of intimacy slipped away suddenly.

Standing behind her was a pale Kathryn.

Sam dropped the balloon in his hand. "Oh, damn." He knew Kathryn wouldn't have come unless... He shot an accusatory look at Erin. "You told her?"

"Don't be angry at her," Kathryn said quickly. As Erin stepped back into the kitchen, Kathryn lingered at the doorway as if uncertain about taking another step. "Is it all right that I came?"

Immediately protective instincts surfaced to make the moment easier on her. "You've always been welcome here."

"You're being very gracious. May I speak to you alone for a moment?"

He heard the strain in her voice and bridged the distance to her.

"Erin told me everything." As if she'd been hit, Kathryn lifted her chin a notch. "About what happened after Erin left town and she called home. I know about Jill's deceit, about the man, about the night she died."

He needed no more from a woman he cared about as much as he would his own mother. "Kathryn, you're here. That's all I care about." With something near despair, he wished he could hug her.

"I'll never understand why she was so jealous of Erin. Jill was so pretty herself, so bright, so popular."

Determined not to let this chance for closeness with her elude him, he spoke words he'd have said to her when Jill had died. "I'm sorry that I couldn't make her happier."

Her eyes swimming with tears, she gave her head a shake. "Perhaps no one would have."

Sam took the first step and folded her in his arms.

Her shoulders raised as if a weight had been lifted from them. "Oh, I'm so sorry," she said fiercely.

For a long moment, he hugged her. "Me, too."

Slowly she drew back. As if a little dazed, she worked up a weak smile. "I owe you a lot of pineapple upside-down cakes, don't I?"

To ease the concern from her face, Sam laughed. "I'll hold you to that."

Despite tears in her eyes, she smiled wider. "So what do you want us to do to help?" she asked while fishing a tissue from her purse.

"Blow up balloons."

"Oh." Between dabbing the tissue at her cheeks, she laughed. "I'm not very good at that."

"Well, do your best." He moved toward the door. "I'll get your windy daughter in here to do most of them."

"I heard that." Erin's gaze cut from his smile to her mother's. "We'd better get busy. We're running out of time."

They had barely finished hanging the decorations when Sara returned home.

Wide-eyed, she stared at the balloons and streamers. "It's so pretty. My favorite colors are..." Her face brightened. "Grandma! You came." She rushed to Kathryn and wrapped little arms around her. "I wanted you to come."

Kathryn blinked quickly before drawing back to smile at her. "I'll be coming to see you a lot now."

"You will?" Sara's eyes darted to Sam.

"A lot," he assured her.

She hugged Kathryn again. "This is going to be the very best birthday."

In response to the ring of the doorbell, Sara raced to the door to greet her guests. Noise and bedlam followed. With Rory's help, Sam directed games while Erin and her mother set out the cake and scooped out ice cream.

Taking a breather while jabbering five-year-olds dug into the food, Erin dropped to the closest chair.

Her eyes dancing, Sara scurried to her. "I knew you'd keep your promise."

There were moments when Erin had had her doubts. "I'm glad you're here."

Erin squeezed her in her arms. Never had she expected to experience a moment like this. Never.

With Erin's kiss, Sara excitedly rushed off to rejoin her guests.

"And I'm glad I'm here," Erin said softly to herself.

Nearby, slouched on a sofa cushion, Sam grinned. "It feels good to sit down." His reprieve lasted only until a freckle-faced boy who Erin learned was Timmy scoffed down the last of his cake. Sam sprang to a stand and popped back into the room to play referee as Timmy pushed another boy, who in turn pushed back. "Game time," he yelled and rolled his eyes at Erin.

Laughing, she disappeared for clean-up duty. With the final paper plates and cups tossed into a bag, she wandered back into the living room and joined Sam to scoop up wrapping paper.

"I forgot something about you." Before she took another step, he curled an arm around her waist.

"What's that?" she asked, smiling as one of the little boys pinned a donkey's tail into a cushion of a chair.

"You're a blabbermouth."

Erin slanted a grin at him. "Guilty."

Discreetly he kissed the sensitive flesh near the shell of her ear. "Thank you."

"Oh." She responded to his lopsided grin and snuggled closer. "Is that a token of things to come?"

"You haven't seen anything yet." he teased, keeping her against him. He smiled at a sight he'd thought could only exist in his imagination—Sara cuddling close to her grandma and showing her one of her presents. For the happiness Erin had given his daughter, he doubted he'd find an adequate thank-you.

Sam purposely waited until the party guests dwindled down to only family. In the excitement of the past few hours, Sara hadn't noticed she hadn't received a gift from him. He disappeared outside with a plan to surprise her. The second he opened the door, the mutt had other ideas. Wiggling his way between him and the door frame, the puppy bounded into the room, then tumbled onto Sara's lap.

Her eyes rounding, she abandoned the balloon in her hand. It floated to the ceiling. "My dog? Is he my dog?" she asked between giggles and the pup's licking. She whipped a look back at Sam, her eyes suddenly brighter. "Is he really mine?"

"He's all yours."

Sara stuck her nose in dog's fur. "You said not till I was a big girl."

"You are, aren't you?"

Beaming, she wrapped her arms around the dog. "Oh, Daddy, this is the best birthday."

What else could he want to hear? he wondered.

"You softie," Erin teased quietly.

One more thing and his life would be perfect, he decided. "Now, you know what you have to do, don't you, Sara?"

Her head bobbed. "Feed him. But you have to give him water 'cause I can't reach the sink."

"What else?" he asked, wanting to remind her that the dog needed to be let outside.

She hugged the dog close again and was rewarded with a sloppy kiss. "Love him."

Sam determined she'd zeroed in on what counted the most. "Sounds right to me."

Kathryn drew closer to the circle of man, woman, child and dog. "Doesn't look like she'll forget that one."

"I'm going to be a dog doctor when I'm bigger," she announced.

"Last year, she wanted to be a butterfly," Kathryn said.

Sam laughed. "No, that was two years ago." Humor laced his voice. "Last year, she wanted to be Reba McEntire." He stared down at Sara and Erin oohing over the puppy.

Watching his child and the woman he loved, he thought nothing could ever be wrong again. Providing a stable home for Sara wasn't enough. She needed the love and laughter Erin had given both of them. But would she give up all she'd found elsewhere? "What are you two up to?" he teased.

Sara giggled. "We're planning a surprise for tomorrow."

"Lucky me." Squatting beside Erin, he murmured softly in her ear, "What about later?"

She released a smoky laugh filled with a promise and tossed a ball of wrapping paper at him. As he caught her arm and tumbled her to the rug with him, Sara flew at Sam. The excited puppy followed, piling on top of them.

Chapter Ten

He'd have liked her to stay the night. She'd refused, uneasy about being there when Sara awakened. Sam figured they could have worked something out, but he couldn't fault her for thinking of Sara first.

If he loved someone, he wanted the woman to win his daughter's heart. He knew he couldn't be everything to Sara. It was something he'd accepted long ago. No matter how close they were, he could never take the place of a mother. He wanted someone Sara could turn to when he wasn't enough.

He'd worked hard to give her a sense of family. It wasn't an easy task for a single parent. Always there was too much to do. Their very survival had depended on his work. He'd known days of feeling as if he was being pulled in a hundred different directions.

No person could escape that feeling if they had to wear too many hats. Somehow, he'd managed to find time for the laundry, the housecleaning, the cooking. And how often had he chauffeured five four-year-olds to preschool?

The house wasn't always as clean as he'd like it to be, dinner wasn't always as balanced as experts insisted, and sometimes he had to hunt to find Sara a matching clean sock or himself a clean shirt. But they were happy. Damn, but he'd wanted that most for her.

He'd known what it was like to live in a perfect house with immaculate surroundings, sit at the dinner table faced with the choice of more than one fork, but never to have shared one laugh with his own father. After Jill had died, he'd vowed his daughter would never know a day without laughter. Children were supposed to be happy and smiling. He didn't doubt he made mistakes, but he was doing his damnedest.

Until recently, he'd given little thought to himself. Sure, he'd been lonely. There were times when he'd fought a restlessness within himself, when he'd needed adult conversation, when he'd longed for a woman beside him in bed. But he'd always felt Sara had to come first. Suddenly there was another person fitting into the picture, and he wondered if he was asking for too much, if it was possible to have it all.

Buttoning his shirt, Sam shuffled out of the bathroom with the puppy trailing. Sara had provided an early wake-up call, leaping onto his bed just after daybreak.

Showered and dressed, he ambled into his bedroom to the sight of her lifting the puppy onto the bed. "You'd better change. Didn't you and Aunt Erin say something about a surprise?"

She rolled over onto her stomach, and with one finger, stroked the puppy's nose. "I wish Aunt Erin was here all the time."

Tossing the towel in his hand to a nearby chair, he dropped to the mattress beside her. "Sara, we have to talk."

Shifting, she turned large blue eyes up at him.

"I know you like her...."

Scooting up beside him, she leaned into his chest and shook her head.

Sam couldn't believe he'd been misinterpreting the growing affection between them. "What? Why don't you?"

"I love her. Do you?" she wanted to know.

He wondered if she'd always be so blunt. He could visualize conversations about babies and birth control and, oh, hell ... "Yes, I do."

Sara cuddled closer. "Will she be my mommy?"

An ache rushed through him. How could he guarantee that to her when he wasn't sure himself? "Sara, she doesn't live here."

"She could." He watched her small chest heave. "Doesn't she love us?"

God, this wasn't easy. More than anything, he didn't want his daughter hurt. "It's not that."

"Daddy?" Deep concentration drew in her brows. "You won't leave?"

He caught the anxiousness in her voice that signaled tears. "No, not me. But you might someday."

She shook her head. "Uh-uh."

He saw no point in confusing her more.

"I wish she'd stay. Then we'd be a family like Tammy's." She ran a hand down his jaw. "You're sticky."

"Like a porcupine?" he asked to lead her thoughts elsewhere while he nuzzled her neck.

She shrieked and squirmed. Laughing, she wiggled, burying her face in the mattress.

"Give?"

He laughed as he heard her muffled, "I give."

Erin thought *she* was the one providing the surprise. Amused, she stood at Sam's kitchen doorway and bit back a smile.

Straddling a chair, he sat behind a stool, combing Sara's hair.

Her eyes shining, Sara looked pleased. "Aunt Erin, hi. You wore your hair like this," she pointed out. "See, I'm just like you."

What she saw was Sam Stone expertly French braiding his daughter's hair. "You have many talents."

Over Sara's head, he feigned a scowl. "You'd better be talking about something else."

Bracing a hip against the counter, she smiled. "Oh, yes, that, too."

"All done." He swung a leg over the chair and turned it back into the table. "So what's the surprise?"

"You'll see," Sara sang and jumped off the stool.

"You'll love it," Erin assured him.

"This is crazy," Sam grumbled, trudging beside Erin through the snow, but he felt like laughing. She'd always done that to him. No man could ignore her beauty, but it was her joy of life that had always captivated him.

"No, it isn't." Erin looked to Sara for reinforcement. "Is it?"

"No, it's fun. We never went on a picnic in the snow before, especially a breakfast picnic."

Trotting along beside her, the puppy swished his tail in agreement.

"I'm outnumbered," Sam said good-naturedly. He'd have gone anywhere she'd suggested, willingly seizing every moment he could have with her, every moment the three of them could share. "What did you bring to eat?"

Sara plopped down on her knees beside Erin. "Lots of good stuff."

Joining them on the blanket, Sam lifted the lid of the picnic basket. He peered inside but played a guessing game with her. "Do you know what's in here?"

Her grin impish, Sara nodded.

Sam leaned back on an arm. "And you made suggestions?"

Again, she nodded.

"Okay. Let me guess. Olives?" Reflectively he stared at the nearby woods blanketed with snow. "Peanut butter-and-jelly sandwiches. Uh..." Sam fastened his gaze on the lid of the basket as if he had X-ray vision. Beside him, the puppy nuzzled its nose under his elbow. "Dog biscuits."

Sara giggled. "You're right."

Sam shot a distressed look at Erin. "Tell me I'm not?"

Laughing, Erin paused in pouring coffee from the thermos and dug into the basket to produce a buttered croissant.

"Thank you." Again the puppy nuzzled him. "This is for me, big guy." He took a bite of the roll. "Sara, you have to give this dog a name."

"Dog."

"No, a name," Sam mumbled between bites, accepting a proffered cup of coffee.

She popped a second olive in her mouth. "Aunt Erin said she had a dog named Lady."

Sam glanced at the pup. "Lady was a girl dog, Sara. This is a boy dog."

"Mister."

"Mister?"

Prone beside him, the pup's tail wagged, swishing his backside.

Over the rim of her cup, Erin's eyes danced. "It's a wonderful name."

While they ate fruit and croissants and hard-boiled eggs, Sara rattled on about a new boy in the neighborhood. "A big boy—his name is Daniel—he knocked down our snowman." Done with eating and growing restless, she stood and shuffled her boots through the snow. She kicked at it, venting her annoyance.

Erin took her cue. "Then we'll have to build another one. A bigger one."

Looking pleased, Sara leaned against Sam's back and wrapped her arms around his neck. "When we go home, we're going to make cookies, aren't we?"

Sam swiveled a look back at Sara.

"You said so," Sara reminded him in a singing voice. "You said the day I didn't go to school we'd make them."

She'd neatly backed him into a corner.

"Remember?"

"I remember." He also remembered he had three loads of laundry to do.

"So that means today. Right?"

With his knuckle, he brushed her nose. "Right."

She beamed at Erin. "Want to help?"

The idea of watching Sam Stone make cookies definitely appealed to her. "I wouldn't miss it."

Sara's smile deepened. "We could make two kinds. Aunt Erin can help make one kind, while you help make the other kind. Then I can take some to school." A deadly serious expression settled on her face. "It's *my* turn."

"Why does she always make sense?" he muttered as Sara danced off through the snow. Balling a napkin, he nudged himself to a stand. As Sara plowed through the snow with the puppy close at her heels, Sam charged and lifted her, stirring her squeal.

Emotion crowding her, Erin watched them tossing snow at each other while the puppy zigzagged in between them and the snow flew in the air. Just as quickly, her heart tightened as if to remind her of a similar happiness she'd once known—and of the agonizing pain.

It was so dumb, so absolutely dumb, but her throat constricted with the threat of tears. Turning away, she began collecting used napkins. While she gathered up the blanket, she struggled with feelings that were so strong, so intense, that if she dropped her guard for a second they'd overwhelm all the logic, all the certainty, she'd had in her life.

"Where are you?" Coming up behind her, Sam slid his arms around her waist to draw her back against him. He smelled her fragrance. Flowers of summer mingled with the winter air.

Erin raised her face to the crisp air, to the snowflakes, light and unhurried, suddenly filtering down around them. The beauty of a whitewashed blue sky blended into snowcapped mountains. A door was opening, the one that had locked when her daughter had died, but she wasn't ready to go through it. "I like being here again," she said, afraid to admit more.

By late afternoon, the kitchen looked like a cookie factory. Sam cast a glance at Sara. She reached for what he thought, if he'd counted right, was her seventh cookie. Beside her, Erin brushed away flour from her cheek and resumed packing the cookies into a tin.

He wanted her in his life. Intimacy offered only a hint of closeness. Lots of people chanced that but refused the final step. She'd never even indicated she might stay. She'd never said words he wanted to hear. At first, they'd spent time together mostly because of Rory. Then she'd come around to his house, several of those times to see Sara. Kathryn's words, that Erin wanted to be close to Sara, not him, played back in his mind. Hell, a woman didn't go to bed with a man if she only cared about his child. That made no sense. But what did she feel? he wondered.

"Can I have another cookie?"

Rousing himself from his thoughts, Sam checked the clock. "No, after dinner."

"Just one?"

"No," he answered, already hunting in the refrigerator for something to cook. "You'd better get cleaned up."

On a huffy breath, she whirled around and out of the room.

Erin stepped close to peer over his shoulder. "What's for dinner?"

"Beats me," he said, hating always having to make this decision.

She smiled at the scowl he was directing at a pound of hamburger. "I'll cook."

Gratitude laced his voice. "You'll cook?"

Laughing, she squinched up her shoulder in response to the soft caress of his lips on her neck. "I don't need convincing."

"Ah, come on, resist a little."

"I'm clean." Sara rushed in, holding her hands in the air for inspection.

Stepping back, Sam grinned at his daughter's timing. "That's more than I can say for this room." He swept a look around the kitchen. "Looks like we've got KP duty."

"That means kitchen police," Sara informed Erin.

Erin nodded. "What's with the we?" She scanned the bowls stacked by the sink, the flour dusting the counter, the egg yolk dripping over it.

"You wouldn't desert me," Sam said.

"Oh, yes, I would," she teased. "I promised Sara a game of Go Fish."

Sara's eyes rounded. "She did," she agreed, bobbing her head emphatically.

"Two against one isn't fair."

Sara giggled behind her hand.

"Oh, all right," Erin conceded. "We'll help."

"Can we watch a movie after dinner?" Sara asked excitedly, hopping from foot to foot. "The one about the mermaid? I like that movie, do you?"

Erin touched her niece's head. "I like it."

"Daddy likes it, too. I'll get it out of the cabinet."

As she took off, Erin heard Sam's low groan. She sidled close to him, bringing her mouth near his ear. "So you like that one, too?" With a turn of her head, she brushed her mouth over his.

Against her lips, he growled low. "Nice. What was that for?"

"Just because." *Because you make me smile, make me laugh.*

"This is the best part," Sara said with a yawn. Her eyes remained on the television screen while she fidgeted closer in Erin's embrace.

In less than five minutes, she was sleeping.

Staring at the child in her arms, she felt her throat tighten and nestled Sara even closer. As one small hand curved over hers, memories penetrated her mind.

When she'd gotten pregnant, she hadn't complained about the exhaustion or the swelling breasts or even the bout or two with nausea. She'd simply been thrilled. From the first flutter to the first kick of the child growing inside her, each stage of pregnancy had brought something new and more wonderful into her life. God, but she'd wanted a child.

Then Lisa had been born. Small and wrinkled with skin that felt rubbery, she'd been beautiful, wonderful, God's miracle. Though her marriage had already taken a turn down a shaky road, Erin had felt a serenity in her life, a fulfillment nothing in her career had ever come close to. She'd never felt so much love before.

Bending her head, she rubbed her cheek across Sara's silky hair and listened to her soft, even breaths. She'd always wanted a family. To her, it had seemed more important than any career. But that dream was gone, would always be gone now.

Sam shifted, sliding his arm off her shoulder. "Let me put her to bed."

With his words, reluctantly she relinquished Sara to him. Just as hesitantly she followed him to Sara's bedroom doorway. She couldn't go in. Too aware she was teetering at the brink of emotion, she didn't want to be a part of the bedtime ritual.

The room was decorated in pink and white and green and filled with a little girl's treasures—stuffed animals, a doll house—and revealed a propensity for ballerinas, from the miniature one on a music box to the exquisite doll propped on a small white end table.

Deep in sleep, Sara didn't stir while Sam slipped her arms out of her sweatshirt, slid off her shoes and tugged off her corduroys. He snatched a deflated-looking beagle from the small white bedside table and took out the pajamas stuffed inside. "Give me a hand, will you?" he asked without a look back.

Refusal seemed impossible. On legs that didn't feel like her own, Erin joined him at the bed.

With their struggle to put on her pajamas, Sam smiled. No smile came back. Silent, too quiet, Erin seemed somewhere else. "What's wrong?"

She straightened to a stand while she fought images of the past. "Wrong?" She spoke quietly, not wanting to wake Sara.

"You hold her," he whispered. "Lovingly. But you look sad."

Dodging his stare, she turned away to fold Sara's clothes.

"Erin?"

She knew he was close behind her even before he'd spoken. How many deep breaths would it take to relax? she wondered. The past shadowed her, seeped in until she could hardly breathe. "Sometimes it hurts," she admitted softly.

He couldn't say what he felt at the moment besides confusion. "What does?"

"Being with her," she said, facing him. "That sounds so selfish, so foolish, but I couldn't see her before this. I couldn't..."

He watched her swallow hard. Sorrow. Waves of it floated over him.

Because she knew he wouldn't let her back away now, she forced words forward. "I didn't tell you everything about my marriage. It ended one night. Simply ended."

Need rippled through him for contact with her. Taking her hand, he slowly led her into the living room. A lamp in the corner of the room sliced light across a portion of her face. Sam urged her down to the sofa and squinted to see her eyes because her voice had sounded so flat.

Erin drew a deep breath. "I didn't lie. There were bad times in my marriage, but I kept hoping. One night, I couldn't find anything more to hope for. We'd gone out to a party. He'd been drinking, so I told him I'd drive. He was furious with me. He refused to give me the keys." Torment darkened her eyes. "Later I learned there had been an accident. He escaped with a broken arm but nothing more." A tremor moved through her. "But our baby died."

Sam didn't move. He couldn't. Shock stopped his heartbeat. "No one told me."

And she hadn't wanted to talk about it. Even when raw with fresh grief, she'd kept the pain private. She pressed her fingertips to her eyelids. She wouldn't cry. Years had passed since that fatal night, a night when a door had seemed to slam in her face. A door she'd been afraid to reopen. "He'd stopped and picked Lisa up from the baby-sitter. At the end of the block, he ran a red light, and the car was broadsided by a truck. She was so small, so innocent."

Dry-eyed, she forced more words. "For so long, I couldn't be around children. Isn't that sad? But I couldn't," she said brokenly. "I kept seeing her face. It seemed to get worse instead of better. Sometimes I'd wake up in the middle of the night, and I'd sit on the bed for a long moment before I realized I wasn't in the home I used to be in, her bedroom wasn't down the hall."

She needed a moment, but one or a dozen wouldn't help. Memory stirred the agony, the unbearable emptiness that had made her insides feel hollow.

Staring at her pale face, he damned the man, every person who didn't comprehend what he'd learned since Sara was born. There was no greater treasure.

No words would help, or at least Sam couldn't imagine any. A woman couldn't lose a child and not be affected by it. Touching Erin's shoulders, he felt her tremble, felt her anguish seeping into him with such intensity that it took effort to breathe. As he gathered her close, he wondered how she'd managed to go on, how she'd adjusted.

He no longer simply held her. He gripped her to him, wishing he could ease her suffering. But he sensed sympathy would mean nothing. It didn't heal, it didn't fill the barren spot where the heart had been.

For a long moment, they clutched each other. At what point she no longer needed his comfort she couldn't say. One moment she was leaning on him, the next she was leaning into him. With darkness descending on them, she coiled her arms around his neck, sought his mouth. Desperately she wanted him, needed him simply to remind her that she was still alive.

* * *

Sam lay in a jumble of sheets. With Erin's face on his chest, he angled his head to stare at her. Emotions flooded him. Why hadn't she told him before this? She'd been through so much, too much pain.

Life threw curves no one expected, he mused. What if they'd never parted? If they'd been together, she'd have never endured that heartache. But she'd never have known her Lisa. And he'd have never had Sara. Merely thinking that sliced a pain through him that was so physical he nearly winced.

No, they couldn't change what had happened, only what might happen. A connection had begun. Perhaps, a new start for both of them. Two people couldn't spend so much time together and not feel it. If he had been the one to always instigate it, he'd think differently, but she'd shown similar needs to be with him ever since they'd returned from their trip. If she wasn't feeling the same, then why would she have done that? There could be no other reason.

His heart stilled for a second. Unless...unless she'd been drawn into his world because he could offer what she'd lost—a child. The thought stung, made him grip her tighter. To believe that meant pushing her away.

He couldn't, not when he could effortlessly imagine waking every morning with her, enjoying the sight of her bathed in the soft glow of morning sunlight. Lightly he toyed with the tips of her tousled hair, then bent his head to brush his lips across her brow. "Awake?"

What sounded like a pleasurable sigh slipped from her lips. "Uh-huh."

Her mind still clouded with sleep, she turned lazily in his arms. Strong, hard thighs pressed against hers. With the graze of his fingers over her hip, she shifted to look up at him. "We don't have time for this, do we?"

He thought they did.

Again, her eyes closed, in response this time to the caress of his lips at the curve of her neck. "What time does Sara wake up?"

"We have enough time."

He'd have liked to stay in bed with her, to linger in the shower, to spend the day doing nothing but staring at her, loving her. Reality took precedence. Ambling down the hallway, he peeked into Sara's room. Curled up, her knees high to her chest, she was buried up to her neck under the blankets. He noticed that she'd abandoned her baby doll. Snug against her was the stuffed black dog Erin had sent her. At the foot of the bed, her new puppy opened one eye at him.

Sam strolled into the kitchen. By the time he finished setting the table, let the puppy outside and back in, the coffeemaker hissed behind him. Sam hefted a frying pan onto the stove and poured milk in a pitcher for Sara's cereal, then strolled to her bedroom.

Quietly he entered the room and moved to her bed. "Hey, sleepyhead."

Her nose red from a cold, she slowly opened her eyes. "I wasn't sleeping."

She could have fooled him.

"I was just real quiet."

Bending forward, he kissed her forehead. "Well, we have company."

Her eyes widened. "Who?"

"Aunt Erin."

She bounced to her knees on the mattress. "Is she having breakfast with us?"

"Yep." Sam waited while she bounded from the bed and wiggled her feet into her cowboy boots.

"Give me a piggyback ride."

"You give me one," he teased, pulling her back between his legs.

She squealed as he leaned against her. "You're too heavy."

"Is that so?" With her smiling face turned up to him, he caught her arm and hefted her to his back.

Erin had hurried. It was one thing to spend the night with Sam, and quite another for Sara to find Aunt Erin in her father's bedroom. Guessing she had only minutes, she carted her clothes into the bathroom, deciding it was a safer place to dress. When she'd been younger, her biggest concern had been her parents' disapproval. Amazingly, one little urchin now had her sneaking around like a skittish teenager. After giving her hair a quick brush, she opened the bathroom door.

Sara stood outside it, the puppy flopped on the rug beside her. "Morning," she said throwing herself at Erin's legs.

Crouching down, Erin welcomed the tight hug. "Good morning to you."

"I got a piggyback ride here," she said in a nasal tone.

Erin thought about mentioning her cold, but she didn't seem hampered by it. "Oh, you're lucky. I had to walk."

She angled close again and whispered in Erin's ear. "I'll ask him to give you one, too."

Laughing, Erin smoothed out Sara's twisted collar. "No, I like to walk."

"Better than piggyback rides?"

"Sometimes." She let her gaze veer from the bright orange flannel pajamas, over the yellow butterflies dancing across the fabric, to her niece's cowboy boots. "I like your boots."

Pulling back, she stared down at the white, slightly scuffed, fringed boots. "Daddy says I'd wear them to bed if I could." She wagged her head. "I wouldn't do that." She looked around Erin. "I got to go in there. Will you wait?"

"I'll wait." Leaning back against the wall she couldn't help thinking how wonderful it must be to see that face every morning. Sara was like a ray of sunshine. Special. She was a terrific little girl who liked snowmen and butterflies and chocolate chip cookies, who cuddled without hesitation, who chattered endlessly with a warmth and friendliness that would touch anyone's heart.

At the click of the door, Erin looked up to see Sara peeking out at her. "Want to brush my hair? Tammy's mommy does hers," she said, handing Erin a small white brush. "But I don't have a mommy, so Daddy always does the back for me."

Squeezed with her in the bathroom in front of the mirror, Erin stroked the brush down long, silky dark strands.

"I wish..." As Sara raised on tiptoes to see her reflection better, Erin noted the wistfulness that had clouded her usually sparkling eyes. "I wish I had a mommy."

It took effort to continue brushing. "You like being with your daddy, don't you?"

She bobbed her head enthusiastically. "But he needs a mommy, too. Tammy's daddy has a mommy he sleeps with. They laugh a lot, too. And they kiss." She gave Erin a broad grin. "I like watching them."

"They kiss because they love each other."

"Do you kiss Daddy?"

Erin sensed she was treading on delicate territory. "Yes, I have."

"Do you love Daddy?"

Turning Sara to face her, Erin wondered how to explain without getting Sara's hopes up. "Do you love Tammy?"

"Uh-huh. She's my best friend."

"Well, your daddy's my best friend." A look far too serious for someone so young settled on Sara's face. Erin poked a tickling finger at her stomach. "Isn't it empty in there?"

She giggled. "Do you like Dinosaur Crackles?"

"Can I think about that one?" Erin asked, taking her hand.

Chapter Eleven

"You have two choices," Sam said as woman and child came into the room with the puppy tailing them. It took an effort not to just stare at them and let the pleasure of the sight wash over him. "Eggs or Dinosaur Crackles?" He held up a box of cereal.

"She's thinking about the Dinosaur Crackles," Sara said helpfully.

Erin gave Sam a discreet shake of her head. "Toast is enough."

"Not in my kitchen," Sam announced, sounding offended. "I'm teaching my daughter the right way to start her day. One or the other."

Sara danced before her. "Have Dinosaur Crackles."

"Eggs," Erin conceded, not missing his satisfied grin.

Sara swung open the refrigerator door. "We don't have apple juice 'cause I don't like it." Little hands gripped the huge carton of orange juice. "Do you?"

"Sometimes."

Sara squinched her nose as she set down the orange-juice carton in front of Erin. "Do you want orange juice?"

"No, thank you."

"You have to have orange juice," Sara informed her in a serious tone. "Doesn't she, Daddy?"

"Yup."

"Like father, like daughter?" Erin murmured, offering a helpful hand on the juice carton while Sara poured from it into a glass.

He shot a smug look at her. "Well trained." Behind him, he heard Sara back in the refrigerator. "No olives for breakfast," Sam said without even looking back.

With a huge sigh, Sara closed the refrigerator door, a tiny pout bowing her mouth. The mood lasted less than a second. Smiling again, she came back to the table to pour cereal into a bowl. "Timmy brought a dead spider to school, and we had yukky cupcakes with green frosting that Kimberly Sue Deekin's mother made."

She scooped up the dinosaur-shaped bits that had overflowed onto the table and dropped them into an already too-full bowl. "I ate one," she confirmed. "'Cause it's good manners." She shook her head. "But I didn't like it. It tasted funny, like toothpaste."

Erin scooped scrambled eggs onto her fork. "They were probably mint flavored."

"Uh-huh." She set down her spoon, letting it slip into the last of the milk and cereal in the bowl. "I go to dancing school today."

"No, you go to school first," Sam prompted, setting a dirty plate in dishwater.

"I know," she returned, sounding a little annoyed at his reminder.

"What if I drive you to school this morning?" Erin asked, certain by the stack of papers she'd seen on Sam's desk that he had a busy day ahead of him.

Because his daughter was nodding happily, Sam didn't contest her offer. But plunging his hands into the dishwater, he frowned. It made no sense but he felt unnerved by Erin's eagerness to be with Sara. Doubts that he'd only given a cursory thought to before nagged at him. Since he'd learned she'd lost a child, he was irritated by Kathryn's words to him about Erin's need for Sara.

Sara's eyes danced with a smile. "Will you go to dancing school with us, too, Aunt Erin?"

"Oh, that sounds like fun."

They smiled at each other, then at him. Sam grappled to match their expression. What if she was transferring to Sara feelings for the child she'd lost? If so, where did he fit into her life?

Too excited about her first dancing class later that day, Sara left for school reluctantly. The image of her hand tucked in Erin's as they strolled to her car lingered with Sam when he wandered into his office to catch up on his work. He fought his own insecurities. The Erin he remembered was honest to the core, too honest to do that. But then the girl she'd been wasn't the woman who'd lost a child.

Not liking his own thoughts, he forced himself to concentrate on work. For a man prone to organization, Sam dealt with a paper-stacked desk that was best described with one word—chaos.

He managed two hours of undisturbed work when Dorothy appeared in the office doorway.

"That leak under the sink is now a flood."

"You're kidding?"

She hadn't been. Together, they mopped the floor. A toolbox in his hand, he returned to the kitchen to the ringing telephone. In no mood for conversation with anyone, he barked a hello.

"Oh, we're grumpier."

Amazingly his mood gentled with the sound of Erin's voice. Shoving a bucket under the pipe, he braced his back against the opened door of the cabinet. "I'm fixing a leaky pipe."

"Would you like me to pick up Sara?" she asked in a light, amused tone that was meant to carry enough sympathy to soothe him.

He should have been pleased by her concern, but he wasn't.

"Sam?"

He focused more intently on her. "Okay."

"See you in a little while," she said brightly.

*   *   *

All Erin saw when she and Sara entered the kitchen were Sam's denim-clad legs stretched out from the cabinet under the sink.

Sara knelt on the floor and peered at him. Rubbing the back of her hand at a dripping nose, she sniffed. "Hi, Daddy."

He grunted a response back at her.

Unsure of his mood, Erin stepped over his one leg and around the other bent one and suggested, "Sara, why don't you get your new sticker book? And I'll pour you some milk."

"Cookies, too?"

Erin ruffled her hair. "Cookies, too."

Disappearing into the other room, Sara fortunately avoided hearing Sam's mumbled curse.

Erin hunched over, trying to see him.

He swore ripely as he hit his knuckle on a pipe.

"Oh-oh." The dog trailing her into the room, Sara covered her mouth. "Did you say a bad word?" she yelled, crouching down to look at him.

"No, I did *not* say a bad word," Sam said defensively.

"I'll get my toolbox."

Erin had the good sense to stifle a grin.

"Daddy bought me this. See?" She wiped the back of her hand at a dripping nose, then set a small plastic tool chest containing plastic wrenches on the table in front of Erin. "Want to borrow one of mine?" Sara peeked under the sink, then crawled under it with him. "Daddy, you're all wet."

Erin couldn't resist. She squatted down to see Sam, more than the leak.

Water squirting at him, he gritted his teeth while he leaned into the wrench again.

Sara mimicked the sound of the water streaming out. "It's really squirting, isn't it, Daddy?"

"Yes, Sara," he said with a patience Erin guessed was costing him as the dog's nosy snout crowded him even more.

From under the sink, metal clanged against metal.

"Got it."

One by one, Erin, the puppy and then Sara backed out from under the sink.

Placing his hands on the sink cabinet, Sam pulled himself forward.

Busy now with milk and cookies, Sara sat at the table with a begging puppy at her side.

"You certainly have enough tools," Erin murmured with a meaningful glance at Sara's bright red toolbox.

"She should know how to do everything." He shrugged before grabbing a rag from the back pocket of his jeans.

As he leaned against the counter and rubbed at stubborn dirt on his thumb, Erin sidled close. A kiss. One kiss helped edge away uncertainties, he realized.

"We're going to be late," Sara said worriedly, breathing in Sam's ear.

"We won't be late," Sam promised his backseat driver. He braked for a stop sign, then turned the final corner and wheeled into the parking lot. He barely flicked off the ignition when Sara burst from the car.

"She's so excited," Erin said, walking with him toward the building.

"I suppose this is just the start of things to come."

Erin patted his shoulder consolingly. "Poor man. Tutus, ballet slippers, are only the beginning. Then there's clothes, always clothes, a dress for a dance, a new sweater, and eventually a wedding dress."

"Old. I'll be old." He opened the door for her. "Stop now."

She laughed, preceding him in.

Even before they entered the school's registration area, the noise of the high-pitched chatter, squeals and giggles of excited four-and-five-year-old girls greeted them.

"Lord," Sam mumbled.

Erin gave him merit points. The only father among at least two dozen women, he actually managed to look at ease during the next few minutes.

"I thought she was too young," he said, smiling at Sara displaying for friends her ability to cross the room on tiptoes. "But the instructor called."

The instructor, a tall, frosted blonde, obviously possessed a flamboyance and flair rarely seen in staid Stony Creek. A red rose had been carefully painted on each dagger-length pink nail. Over black leotards, she wore hot-pink-colored leg warmers that matched her scooped-neck top.

"She said she had others Sara's age and urged me to bring her."

Noting the woman's sly glances in Sam's direction, Erin guessed why.

Sam fixed his gaze on Sara, but his thoughts wandered. With Rory's trial date five days away, he'd calculated that his best defense rode on being able to discredit the prosecution's eyewitness—Don Willis. Sam considered the scene before him. Judging by the milling crowd, the first class wouldn't start for another half hour. "I should visit the Jorgensens."

Her eyes on Sara, Erin prayed one of Lori's neighbors had seen Rory hanging around the Fremont house the night of the car theft. "I'll stay with Sara," she said, anxious for him to go if it meant a possibility of bringing back good news. When he didn't respond, she dragged her gaze away from watching Sara and smiled at him.

He didn't smile back. Instead, something flashed in his eyes.

Puzzled, Erin stared after him. What kind of a look was that? His gaze had hung on her. There'd been no smile, no seduction, only questions in his eyes. If she hadn't known better, she'd have said she'd seen distrust in his eyes. That was silly, of course. Why wouldn't he trust her?

She banished that thought—it seemed ridiculous— and weaved her way to a metal bleacher. A hand on her arm halted her in midstride.

"What are you doing here?" Cheryl Weber unbuttoned her jacket but kept a watchful eye on her daughter, a tall, pudgy six-year-old who looked more eager to run to the door than take lessons.

"Sam enrolled Sara."

Conspiratorially, Cheryl leaned close to her. "Rowena Barnes has the hots for him," she said about the instructor. "It's good you came with him." Curiosity filled the dark gaze she turned on Erin. "Are you two—"

Erin couldn't deny involvement with Sam, but she knew that what they had wasn't permanent, never could be. She doubted, though, that Cheryl, who, at fourteen, had planned a future of a husband, three kids, a house and a cat, would understand.

"Oh-oh, I hear a call for Mommy," Cheryl said distractedly. Her daughter had found a wall to cling to.

Erin produced a slim smile. It would have required too many explanations to set Cheryl straight.

"Without Sam here, Rowena can get down to business now," a voice said behind Erin.

Erin mustered a grin for Tammy's mother, and with her wound a path around clusters of little girls to settle on the bottom bleacher.

Noise shifted Erin's gaze from Sara to the older girls ambling into the room. One in particular caught her eye. "Isn't that Lori Fremont?"

Tammy's mother followed her stare. "Beautiful girl, isn't she? She's in the advanced class. A wonderful dancer, but it always makes me nervous when I know the older girls will be here at the same time." At Erin's quizzical expression, Tammy's mother jerked her head toward the door.

A teenage boy dressed in dirty jeans and an equally soiled black parka slouched against an adjacent wall. "He's always hanging around here when Lori has classes."

Strangely, Erin felt what Tammy's mother hadn't mentioned. The boy's expression was surly, his eyes downright mean and his stare at Lori repulsively lascivious.

"He makes all of the mothers nervous."

As if to punctuate the woman's words, Cheryl sidled close to Erin but never took her eyes off the boy. "That kid gives me the creeps."

Erin noted the boy's chipped front tooth when he presented Lori with a leering smile. Either she didn't notice him or chose not to.

"Isn't she something?" Cheryl shook her head. "I never looked that good at sixteen."

"Does Lori like him?" Erin asked with disbelief as she thought about her brother's interest in the girl.

"I doubt it."

Tammy's mother leaned toward them again. "I was here one time when he pestered her. Grabbed her arm to stop her. She was furious. She told him to leave. He looked so angry, scarily angry. But she didn't back down."

Erin fixed her gaze on him a moment longer. "Who is he?"

"Bobby Willis."

The collar of his jacket raised, Sam slid his way through the icy parking lot. The sound of a piano and a children's song, "Twinkle, Twinkle, Little Star," announced that class had begun.

From the doorway, he sought out Erin, crossed to her quickly, then dropped onto the bleacher beside her.

Eyes shining, Sara followed the line of girls tiptoe-ing around the room and waved at him.

"They started only a few minutes ago," Erin said quietly.

"Oh, damn."

Erin looked up to see the reason for his annoyance.

Sauntering his way, Rowena nearly batted her eye-lashes at him. "You are going to let your daughter take lessons, aren't you?"

"If she wants."

The woman's green shadowed eyes swept over him assessingly.

Sam practically squirmed.

"I'm delighted," Rowena assured him, squeezing his arm meaningfully before turning away.

"Don't," he warned Erin without looking at her as he slouched down on the bleacher again.

Her muffled laugh came out like a snort. "Not me."

Shoulder-to-shoulder with her, he slanted a nar-row-eyed look at her.

She couldn't help herself. She laughed openly.

Believe in her, he told himself. Believe in what's been shared. Because he desperately wanted to, he closed a hand over hers. "I'll get you for this later."

"Is that a threat or a promise?" she teased.

"A fact."

The girls continued in their circular movement around the dance floor.

"Three steps forward, now twirl," Rowena in-structed.

Sam smiled proudly. "She's cute."

"Rowena?"

"No! Sara."

Smiling, Erin nudged him with her shoulder. "You weren't gone long."

"None of the Jorgensens saw anything."

Instead of disappointment, Erin smirked. "I learned something."

A puzzled expression crossed his face. "Where?"

"Here."

"How could you learn anything here to help Rory?"

"I'm observant." Quickly she filled him in on Bobby Willis's obsessive behavior toward Lori Fremont.

"That could be important."

"It is," she insisted, certain they'd finally learned something meaningful to help her brother.

Sam hated jumping to conclusions about anything. "We won't know that until we talk to Rory," he cautioned.

They found Rory in the garage fiddling again with the motorcycle. He shrugged at Sam's question. "Bobby Willis and I had words about her," he admitted. "But Lori never dated him."

"Because of you?" Erin asked.

"And because he's a jerk."

Sam guessed what Erin was thinking. They'd had their own lives disrupted by Jill's manipulations. Logic indicated a possibility that Bobby Willis was reeking havoc with Rory's life. "But he might think you're the reason for her refusal."

"It's possible, isn't it?" Erin asked.

Standing, Rory wiped grease from his hands. "What are you getting at?"

"That he might think eliminating you would help him."

Silent, Erin ambled with Sam into the house. On the sofa, Sara was nestled close to Kathryn and fingering the afghan her grandmother was knitting while chattering about her dance class. Erin felt some satisfaction at seeing Sara, her grandmother and her father all together in one room.

Sam didn't bother to unbutton his coat. "Kathryn, could Sara stay with you for a while?"

"Of course." She paused with her needles.

"We're going to drive back to Concord and talk to Dwayne Mostley."

"Go," Kathryn urged, smiling down at Sara who was counting the rows of stitches. "And don't worry if you get caught in another snowstorm. Sara can stay with me again."

At the door, Erin snuck a look back at her. "It's not snowing."

"Well, you never know if you'll get detained somewhere," she said lightly.

Laughing, Erin stepped outside ahead of Sam. "I don't believe that. My own mother giving me permission to—"

"Yeah," he said on a slow grin. "Always did love that woman," he added, grabbing her hand.

Snow crunched beneath their boots during the walk from the car to the opened shed behind a big white farmhouse. Snow swirled at them from a nearby snowdrift. Puffs of white hung precariously on nearby towering pines, but despite the icy afternoon wind, the sky's blue held no threatening storm this time.

"You could have stayed in the car," Sam said as she shivered beside him.

"No, I couldn't."

He noted the almost imperceptible tilt of her chin to a defiant angle and smiled. "Come on, then, let's hurry inside and—"

"Who's out there?"

A man with a grizzled beard, dressed in a red plaid jacket and a corduroy cap with the earpieces down, stood in the wide doorway of the shed, a rifle in his hands.

Sam made quick work of explaining who they were and why they were there, making sure to drop Harley's name in his explanation at least four times.

"You shouldn't have wasted your time." Mostley leaned his rifle against a wall. "Already gave a description of the man to our sheriff."

Sam asked him to repeat it. Beside him, he heard Erin's distressed sigh as she recognized, too, that the man didn't match Ron Kale's description of Techner. "Young?" Sam asked. "You said he was young. Dark-haired."

Head bent, Mostley squatted beside a disassembled engine. "Yup."

Her heart twisting, Erin hugged herself as much against the chill inside her as protection from the bitter wind blowing through the open doorway. "Good-looking?"

The old man swung a slow look over his shoulder. "Hell, no."

Hope rose in Erin. No one would deny that Rory was good-looking.

"Real dirty. That's one of the reasons I didn't bother with him. Looked like the kind of kid who'd probably stolen everything."

"What about a chipped front tooth?" Erin asked.

Sam swung a look of incredulity at her. "You noticed a chipped front tooth?"

"Women notice things."

"Let's hope one man did, too," he said quietly.

Hunkered down in front of the engine, Mostley scratched the back of his head, tipping his cap forward.

"Did he?" Erin insisted.

"Don't remember."

Discouraged, Erin leaned against Sam.

"You comin' in for supper, Dwayne?" a rotund woman dressed in overalls, a plaid shirt and a heavy olive-colored sweater grumbled from the doorway.

"Keep your pants on. Be right there. These folks needed some help. About that fella who came here trying to dump those parts on me. Remember him?"

Erin whirled around to face the woman squarely. "Did you see him?"

The woman gathered her heavy sweater to her chest. "Sure, I saw him. Ugly kid."

"Chipped front tooth?" Erin asked.

"Sure did have one."

"Don't gloat," Sam said in response to her smug grin when they were strolling back to the car.

"I'm not gloating."

With an arm tight at her waist, he reached around her to open the car door and brushed his lips across her temple. "Go ahead and gloat. It's good news."

Good news. Finally, Erin mused, staying in the car while Sam talked to the sheriff, finally someone had identified Bobby Willis. Sam might have been right. If they proved that Bobby was involved with the car-theft ring, that he sold the parts, then reasonably his father might have diverted blame on Bobby's rival to throw authorities off the track.

Swiveling on his chair, Joe Dunn shook his head at Sam. "Until Mostley's wife IDs Bobby Willis, we don't have anything. A lot of kids have chipped front teeth."

Unwilling to give up, Sam perched on the edge of his desk. "Maybe a little pressure would help."

Thoughtfully Joe stared at him. "Are you asking me to bother that poor boy?"

"Something like that," Sam answered.

Joe smiled slowly. "I might do better than that." He shoved back his chair. "I might bring daddy and son in." He chuckled with private amusement. "Call you if we get news."

Rory growled about Bobby Willis when they told him. "That lousy son of a—"

Kathryn cleared her throat and jerked her head toward Sara to silence him.

"Keep your distance from the Willis family," Sam cautioned.

"Are you paying attention to him?" Kathryn asked Rory. She turned away, then held out a sheet of paper to Erin. "Your agent called while you were gone." Her mother stared expectantly at her. "Will you have to leave soon?"

Sara wandered in, dragging her jacket. "I don't want you to go. Are you leaving?"

Erin acknowledged she hadn't given that a thought. She enclosed Sara in an embrace. "No, sweetheart. Uncle Rory still needs me. I'm not leaving you."

Slowly Sam raised his head. He couldn't stop echoing words from filling his mind. *Erin's only seeing you because of Sara.*

Tears still glistening in her eyes, Sara trotted closer to Sam. "I'm hungry."

Erin laughed. "You're always hungry. Maybe we can talk your daddy into hamburgers."

"Can we?" Sara turned a smile filled with charm up at him.

He wanted to hold on, to ignore all sensible thought for the first time in his life. "With lots of onions," he teased his daughter.

Sara wrinkled her nose. "Phewie."

Pressure in his chest made breathing difficult. He clung to the sight of Erin's smile. He absorbed the sound of her laughter when, with Sara in the car between them, they stopped for hamburgers and milk shakes. He cherished time, wishing he could stop it as they sat in front of his fireplace eating.

Yet apprehension lingered. All day, he'd dealt with doubts. He'd battled to get a grip on them and couldn't. Not once had Erin said she loved him, said she'd wished she'd stayed with him, wanted to now.

When he carried Sara to bed later, pride gnawed at him. He couldn't go on like this. He needed answers, had to have them before he went nuts from thinking too much. "She never stirred," he said, returning to Erin still sitting on the sofa.

Complacent, she had to nudge herself to move. "I suppose I should go home."

A cowardly streak held him silent. He wanted more time with her. Whether or not he was sticking his head in the sand like some dumb ostrich, he stopped her movement toward the door. His hand roaming down her arm, he let her warmth seep through him to soothe his own uncertainties.

"Well, maybe not yet," she murmured in response to his mouth tracing the curve of her jaw. Gently she pushed an elbow into his stomach. "Beat you to the bed," she sang out and rushed toward the steps.

She made it halfway up them before he snagged her waist, then gathered her up in his arms. Laughing, they tumbled onto the bed.

He had to be wrong about everything. He had to be. "Why did we waste so much time?" he whispered.

"Why are we now?" she mumbled before her mouth pressed against his.

The moment was different. With a heady sigh, she closed her eyes. Whispery caresses, gentle strokes. Then hands grew more relentless, kisses became hungrier.

He couldn't think when he was with her like this. Fire and heat pushed aside everything else. With the same swiftness that he slipped clothes from her, she helped him out of his. She hurried him until only the slick texture of damp skin mattered.

He felt no patience. With a wildness he was becoming accustomed to, she matched his intensity now, her tongue gliding across his shoulder, his chest, his stomach.

Her delicate hands scrambled him to the edge of reason. Pleasure rushed him as if he'd never known this closeness before with her, as if her body's softness was unfamiliar.

Desperation. It hounded him as she whispered his name. Her pleasure overshadowing the ache throbbing through him, he caressed and stroked until sanity seemed to be slipping from him.

With his hands on her hips, he guided her, pulled her closer. She snatched every breath he could draw. Where tenderness and exploration had led them before, now an awakening of a different sort raced over him. Love. He clung to it, accepted that it had always been, might always be. Never would there be another for him.

Even as she made him ache, he needed to see her eyes this time, watch her face. Holding back a moan as fire leapt through him, he raised himself above her. Blue eyes, hooded from desire, met his as he entered her. Moist flesh blended. As her arms wrapped around him, as her legs gripped him to her, he caught his breath.

Then breathing no longer mattered. She moved with him. Deeply he drove her until he couldn't think, until muscles trembled. With a quiet shudder, she gripped his shoulders. He had one last thought before pleasure washed over him. It wasn't enough. Then he gave in, not caring about anything but this moment and the sensation sprinting through him.

Was he still breathing? he wondered minutes later. Drawing a shaky breath, he groped his way back to reality.

Poised above her on one elbow, he skimmed a hand over her hip. Slender, delicate, she was fragile—more fragile, he sensed, than she'd ever been. Shadows slanted across her face. Skin he knew, skin he had touched and tasted, looked pale beneath the moonlight spearing into the room. Unwilling to relinquish even a second of closeness, he rolled to his back and drew her against his side.

He didn't remember falling asleep. Awakening to darkness around him, he reached for her.

But she was gone.

Chapter Twelve

Before ten the next morning, Sam resigned himself to having a bad day. Sara awoke coughing. The washing machine vibrated, then droned to a halt, and a repairman drawled unsympathetically over the telephone that it would be a couple of days before he could come to fix it. Sam dropped Sara off at school and made one stop before going home.

Restless, he barely managed to sit through three appointments without losing concentration. Abandoning paperwork, he gave Dorothy directions about a will and headed for the door. He was one step from it when she called him back to answer the phone. That one phone call changed his mood.

* * *

"Good news," he told Erin when she opened the door to him.

At the table, Rory was standing, waiting.

Kathryn rushed forward to stand beside him. "What happened?" she asked anxiously.

Sam couldn't help grinning. "The arrested parts shop owner finally identified the men he got the stolen goods from. According to Ed, the guy was getting nervous about taking the rap by himself."

Beside him, Erin touched his arm. "And Rory wasn't named?"

Sam grinned at her. "No."

"Oh, thank God." Kathryn sighed and hugged her son.

"I'm clear?" Rory asked. "Of everything?"

"You bet," Sam assured him.

"How?" he demanded to know.

"The sheriff learned the identity of one of the men."

"Chipped front tooth?" Erin asked.

Sam squeezed Erin's waist. "Bobby Willis. With that ammunition, Ed confronted Don Willis about his claim that he saw Rory and got him to admit that he lied about it."

A pleased expression swept over her face. "Did he do it because of Bobby's feelings about Rory?"

"Partially." He gave her a wry grin. "As far as Bobby was concerned, Rory was the perfect one to blame. Father and son thought they'd set him up and they'd be off the hook."

"*They'd* be?" Kathryn's eyes widened. "Both Don and Bobby were involved?"

"They've been involved in a lot of car thefts according to their partner-in-crime."

"What about Techner?" Rory asked. "He's for real, isn't he?"

"Don Willis said that Techner is probably in Canada somewhere. But he was part of it, too."

"It's a wish come true." Kathryn hugged Rory again.

"Mom, don't cry." Awkwardly Rory drew her closer in his arms.

As a criminal lawyer in Boston, Sam had found moments such as this one the most satisfying. Smiling at their happiness, he glanced at his wristwatch. He swore softly, drawing only Erin's attention. "I'm late. I have to pick up Sara."

"Come back," she urged, strolling with him to the door.

He kissed her hard and quick. "I'd planned to." Stepping outside, he fingered the ring box in his pocket.

Sam picked up a coughing Sara from school. Concerned, he wheeled the car in the opposite direction. It was nearly four when they left the doctor's office with a prescription and instructions about a humidifier.

Squirming on the seat beside him, Sara fidgeted with her seat belt. Peripherally he caught her tipping her head. "Can I go see Aunt Erin?"

As much as he'd planned on going back there, that was before he'd taken Sara to the doctor. Looking at her, he watched her sniff. "I think you should go home."

"I feel okay." She sniffed again and held up a wrinkled paper. "I want to show her my drawing."

"Okay, but we're not going to stay."

Watery eyes on him, she nodded.

We're both in a bad way for one woman, he decided.

Her eyes droopy, her nose red, Sara looked miserable to Erin. She dropped to Sara's level to unzip her jacket while her mother cornered Sam with questions about legalities. "That's some cold you have."

"Uh-huh," she said in a foggy voice.

"Feel lousy?"

She shook her head, then sneezed twice.

"Maybe you should go to the doctor."

"We did. Daddy said I could only stay for a little while." She held out her drawing. "I wanted to show you."

Erin set her jacket on a chair.

"There's five butterflies. Four big and one small. I'm the small one."

Erin drew her into the circle of her arm.

"We were told to draw our family. I drew my family. See these butterflies. That's Grandma and Rory outside their house. And Daddy, you and me are outside this house," she said, pointing.

Erin's heart clutched. "It's a pretty picture, Sara."

She beamed. "Everyone else drew people." She squinched her nose. "Timmy's people looked like fish.

He said my idea was dumb." She scowled. "I didn't think so."

"Neither do I. I think it's wonderful."

"Can I have some milk?"

Erin ran a hand over her head. "Maybe juice," she answered, thinking it would be better for her than the milk because of her cold.

"And cookies?"

Erin bit down on her top lip as she stared at the drawing. "Of course." Behind her, the phone shrilled. As her mother started for it, Erin grabbed the receiver, aware if she stared at the drawing too long emotion might pour out of her. Offering a greeting to the caller, she noticed her mother step closer to Sam.

"What did the doctor say?"

"He said it's inflammation of the larynx." Because Sara was staring hard, watching him, Sam veiled his concern with a jibe at a tired-looking Rory, "What's your excuse? Late night with Lori?"

Kathryn raised her brows. "Too late."

Sam managed a laugh. Eavesdropping wasn't his style, but he found himself catching snatches of Erin's phone conversation.

"Yes, it is a one-in-a-million opportunity," she said to the caller.

Sam needed no explanation. She'd gotten the commercial. Time for a reality check, he mused. She had another life, but this time, why couldn't they blend both their worlds?

Erin sent down the receiver and faced him. "That was my agent."

"I figured that." He opened his jacket. "Big chance, huh?"

"I still have to audition."

Sara turned a bewildered look on her. "I don't want you to go," she cried, wrapping her arms around Erin's hip.

Erin released a shaky breath and squatted to her level. "Sara, I have a job, just like your daddy does, but mine isn't here." Staring into Sara's sad eyes, Erin could see that nothing she'd say would soothe her.

"Come on, Sara," Kathryn urged gently. "Let's get some cookies."

With the back of her hand, she wiped at tears on her cheeks. Her eyes shifted from Erin to her grandmother.

"I made some this morning. Your favorites."

Clearly she took her grandmother's hand only because it was expected of her, but at the kitchen doorway, she looked sadly back at Erin.

If it were possible, she'd have postponed this moment to avoid seeing that look in Sara's eyes. "Oh, Sam."

"I'll talk to her," he said, closing the distance between them. He understood Sara's agony. He was dealing with his own. He'd always promised himself he wouldn't do what his father had done, wouldn't force his life on the woman he loved. But he needed something to hold on to while she wasn't around. Once before he'd let her leave without telling her what he felt. "She's not the only one who's going to miss you."

A deep churning need swept through her to let those words touch her. She wished she'd heard them years ago, wished she could transcend everything that had happened during the intervening years.

"I want you to come back." This time, he had to say the words that had haunted his soul for years. "I love you, Erin."

She realized she hadn't thought beyond the time she was spending with him. "Sam, I—I don't know what to say."

He'd have thought what she should say would have been obvious. Not getting the response he'd hoped for, he kept himself from moving closer.

Confusion swept over her. During the past weeks, she'd allowed herself moments, happy ones, she realized, but in her heart, she knew she wasn't capable of giving him more. She was too empty inside, too haunted by a despair that was as much a part of her as breathing. How could she think about a future when memories from the past consumed her? "My life isn't here anymore," she said because she couldn't offer any other explanation.

Instinctively his back straightened as if readying for a hard blow. "I know that."

"I never planned not to leave. I'm sorry." She avoided his stare, darkening now with hurt. Hurting him was the last thing she'd ever meant to do. "I haven't been fair to you. Or to Sara. I know she wants a mommy. I know that—"

"We're not talking about Sara," he flung. "We're talking about you and me." A wave of desperation floated across him. He warred with himself and smothered the urge inside him to beg. "Tell me what you feel." *Say you love me.* If she'd say the words, if he could believe in them, he could fight for her.

But she was silent.

The pain was so strong, he felt a soreness in his chest. It wasn't something he'd allow himself to think about until later. He'd married one woman who hadn't loved him, not really. Jill had seen Judge William Stone's son. She'd wanted to live in the house on the hill. Wanted to be a big city lawyer's wife. But she hadn't loved him. He needed a woman who'd love him not for what he could give her but for who he was. He'd been so sure it was different with Erin. "If you don't love me, then what was this between us?" he demanded. "Why have you kept seeing me?"

She felt cornered more by her own feelings for him than his demand. She couldn't handle this now. She spoke from her heart, the truth. "I don't know."

She couldn't have sliced him open more effectively. He stood still for a moment. If she didn't love him, then there was only one other reason. He'd been necessary to her, not because of love but because he'd offered her something valuable she'd lost—a child.

He fought the urge to stop the moment, back up, give them both time to calm down. "Everything between us has been because you wanted to get closer to Sara, hasn't it?"

"No!" She shook her head. "I can't believe you'd even think that."

"I'm thinking a lot worse. I'm wondering if you used my daughter as a substitute."

Shock tore at her, threatening to snatch the breath from her. How could he believe that? She'd loved her own child too much to hurt another child that way.

With the bang of the swinging door, they both jumped.

"I ate..." Sara's voice trailed off. She skidded to a stop, her eyes leaping from Erin to her father. Bewilderment knitted her brows. "Daddy, are you mad?"

Lying to her was something he'd tried to avoid. As Kathryn came back in, he insisted, "It's time to leave, Sara."

She still looked puzzled. Sam mentally prepared himself, aware how persistent she could be.

She opened her mouth. Instead of questioning him, she coughed.

Standing beside her, Kathryn smoothed back the hair at her forehead and soothed, "You just need a good night's sleep." She hugged her grandmother, then her eyes veered to Erin. She hurled herself at her.

With her face in Sara's hair, the scent of lemon filling her, Erin held her for a long moment. Too much emotion closing in on her, she felt entangled in a web of conflict. "I'll miss you." Her eyes went to Sam. *You, too.* But she couldn't give them what they'd need. She simply didn't have any more to give anyone.

"Sara, she'll be back soon to visit," Kathryn said to ease her granddaughter's distress.

Her heart thudding, Erin took the cue. "Yes, I will."

"Hey, kiddo, come on." Sam held out a hand for his daughter. Against his will, he looked at Erin, took a long moment to absorb everything about her to memory. He felt frustration build, the hurt intensify, and turned away before he made a fool of himself.

He'd forget her, he kept convincing himself during the drive home. Silent, Sara rushed into the house ahead of him and up the steps. "Get ready for bed, Sara." It was the first thing he'd said to her since they'd left the house. He couldn't stifle a foul mood. As if sensing it, Sara didn't balk and try to put off her bedtime but scurried up the stairs.

Not flicking on a light, he wandered into the living room and flopped on the sofa. Damn fool. There was no other description for him. With a curse, he took the ring box out of his pocket and flung it across the room. He felt more tired than he'd ever been in his life.

"Daddy?" Sam swiveled his gaze away from the blank television set to Sara standing in the archway. The black dog clutched in her arm, she trotted to him. He forced a numbing calm. What choice did he have? His anger would only frighten her. Above all else, he'd always think of his daughter first.

"Are you sad?" she asked in a hoarse voice. "Me and Blackie are."

He opened his arms to her. When he lifted her on his lap, he ran a hand over her arm as much to offer comfort as to gauge if she felt warm with a fever.

"Why does she have to go?" She covered her mouth and coughed. "I don't want her to go."

Sam saw too much hurt in her eyes—too much pain. If he was hurting, it was his own damn fault, but she didn't deserve this. It took a moment to remind himself the pain was fleeting. Wouldn't it have been worse if Erin had stayed, if she'd become a part of their lives, yet they'd never become a real part of her heart? "She has to."

She pressed her temple against his. "Will she ever come see me?"

God, he could hear himself asking his father the same question about his mother. "Sometimes," he answered because to say anything else would only deepen her sadness.

She lifted her head and touched his face. "Want my Blackie?"

He tightened his hold on her. "No, you keep him," he said in a voice that sounded huskier even to his own ears. "And I'll hug you."

With her every breath, she moaned.

Frowning at her labored breathing, Sam lifted her in his arms. "Come on. Bedtime."

After tucking her in, he spooned out the medicine the doctor had prescribed, gave it to her and plugged in the humidifier. Worried, he ran a hand across tired eyes and settled on a chair in her room, unable to stifle his edginess about her breathing.

Emotionally drained, Erin labored to climb the stairs toward her room. There was nothing left for her to do now except pack. As she wandered down the hallway, she couldn't stop thinking about his last words to her. How could he say those things about Sara? Didn't he know that what she felt for her was genuine?

Lost in thought, she stilled at the sound of a bang. It was then she saw her mother bent over a box in Jill's room. Erin moved to the doorway and stared at the blank walls, at the boxes by the bed filled with Jill's collection of perfume bottles. "Mom?"

She looked up briefly, then resumed wrapping newspaper around each bottle. "I suppose I shouldn't ask, but I would have had to be blind not to see something was wrong when Sam was here."

Everything was wrong. Erin kept the thought to herself. Instead, she gestured toward the boxes. "Mom, what are you doing?"

She heaved an enormous sigh. "What I should have done long ago."

Swaying back against the doorjamb, Erin felt tears for her. She fought them just as she'd blocked the ones that had threatened since the night her own daughter had died. She'd learned if she didn't give in to them, if she rejected emotions that hurt too much, they wouldn't exist. But more than anyone, Erin knew how difficult the task of packing a loved one's possessions was. "Do you need help?"

Her mother rose from her bent position. "No, dear. Thank you, but *I* need to do this." No hesitancy colored her voice. "It's time to let go, to put the past behind me," she said firmly, though there were traces of strain and fatigue in her face.

How could she not admire her mother's bravery? Erin wondered. There was no pain as great as losing a child. Nothing wiped away the void, the loneliness, the yearning to have one more second, just one more to hold your child, to see its smile, to love it. Just one more. One more.

Blinking, she turned away before her mother saw and rushed to her room. She thought about the rattle, the pink dress, the tiny sweater she hadn't had the courage to part with. How could she forget the past? If she did, she'd have nothing left.

So she clung to memories. She remembered the sound of tires screeching when Phillip had pulled away from the curb, leaving her standing on the sidewalk, staring after him. She'd known then her marriage was over.

She remembered the baby-sitter's pale face when she'd arrived at her door for Lisa. She remembered the woman's words. "Your husband came for her."

She remembered the panic that had swept over her after friends had driven her home, and she'd entered a quiet, empty apartment.

She remembered the questions. Where was he? Where was her baby?

She remembered the knock on the door, the policeman. She'd heard words but not sentences. Accident. Husband. Daughter.

She remembered running through the hall of the hospital, a doctor's sad look and the words that had wrenched her heart from her. *Your baby is dead.*

Erin sank onto the bed. The memories had played before her like a filmstrip, the pain shadowing it. Tears slipped out. She couldn't stop them this time. Trembling, she wept. *I miss you, Lisa. I'll always miss you.* Emotion tore at her. It consumed her, forcing her to give in. Pain so fierce she rocked with it swept through her.

Let go of the past, her mother had said. Let go.

Closing his eyes, Sam dozed, but not restfully. He kept stirring, his eyes darting to Sara. Even in sleep, she coughed.

It was a harsher sound that jolted him off the chair and to her bed. A moan accompanied each breath she drew. As her eyelashes fluttered, he felt her forehead. The heat frightened him. "Hey, sweetie."

She peeked at him from eyes opened to slits and rasped words between noisy breathing. "I don't feel good."

Tension knotted his stomach. "Do you hurt?"

"Here," she croaked, touching her chest. A coughing fit grabbed hold, forcing her to sit up. Her eyes widened with alarm. "Dad—dy."

"It's okay," Sam soothed over the harsh barking cough.

The panic gripping him swung into terror before he arrived at the hospital with her. With her cradled in his arms, he rushed into the emergency room.

Let go. With a shuddering breath, Erin brushed tears away. Her chest ached. But the sadness. Oh, God, the sadness that had ripped her apart for so long was finally gone.

She knew memories of Lisa would always be a part of her. She'd never forget the quick tug of a corner of her mouth before she smiled, her struggle to tug off booties, the way she always bubbled out string beans.

Tears still swimming in her eyes, Erin smiled with good memories. It would be better now, she knew. For the first time since her daughter had died, as if she'd been cleansed from the pain, she felt no heaviness inside her.

Standing, she fingered a blouse to pack. On the bed lay the drawing Sara had left with her. A huge sun beamed down on the butterflies. It depicted happiness. Three butterflies. Tracing one of them with a finger, Erin smiled. Happiness had snuck in on her because of another little girl, because of a man who'd touched her heart years ago.

"Daddy, you and me," Sara had said. "I drew my family." *A family.* She saw them as a family. Oh, wasn't that what she wanted most, too?

She sank back to the bed. *Oh, Sam, I'm sorry.* She'd fallen in love with him again, yet hadn't told him. Why she hadn't seemed so obvious suddenly. Grief had locked the love inside her. The realization burned in her throat because she knew now how much she may have already lost. She'd had a second chance. What she'd wanted most had been within her grasp. All she'd had to do was reach for it. Instead, she'd turned away from that happiness and from love.

"Erin, do you want help packing?" When Erin looked up, her mother rushed in. "You've been crying. What's wrong?"

"Nothing."

"Honey." She brushed Erin's cheek. "Are you sure you're okay?"

"Yes. I think I finally am." Erin released a huge sigh. "But what if it's too late to tell Sam?"

Her mother joined her on the bed and curled an arm around her shoulder. "That you love him?" As Erin nodded, her mother smiled. "It's never too late."

"He might not believe me." She had trouble getting the words out. "He thinks everything we shared was because of Sara, that I'd gotten closer to him to spend more time with her, that I was using her to fill some void in my life."

Distress creased the lines in her mother's face. "He said that?" As she nodded, her mother paled. "Oh, he couldn't have believed me." Shaking her head, she took a long moment before meeting Erin's questioning stare. "When you first came back, I told him you were only seeing him because of Sara. Oh, I have no excuse for it except that I wanted to keep him away from you. I'm sorry," her mother said with self-disgust. "I nearly forgot—" The shrill of the telephone whipped her around. "Don't pack anymore until we talk," she insisted before dashing from the room.

Erin closed her eyes, but she could still see the hurt that had been in his. Now she understood why he'd believed that about Sara. This was her fault, not her mother's. She'd given him no reason to think differently. If only she'd told him that she loved him.

"Erin!"

The panic in her mother's voice sent her flying from the room to the top of the stairs.

"Come on," she yelled while shrugging into her coat.

"Where?"

"To Sara." She scooped Erin's jacket from the hall closet. "Sam called. Sara's in the hospital."

In silence, they raced to the hospital. *She's not your child,* her mind screamed. But Sara had become as much a part of her as if she'd come from her own womb. She whipped the car into the hospital parking lot. "Oh, Mom, how could Sara get so ill so quickly?"

It was a thought that lingered while they ran toward the hospital front entrance. Impatience and worry mingled during the elevator ride. When the doors swooshed open, Erin bolted from it to the nurses' station. "Sara Stone," she requested.

"What room?" Kathryn asked from behind her.

"Two-ten."

Their heels clicked at a fast pace on the highly polished tile floor. "Sam said that by the time he got here, she was turning blue around the lips," Kathryn said with a tremor in her voice.

Erin draped an arm around her shoulder. "Mom, she'll be okay." *She has to be.*

The quick pace of footsteps from the hallway reeled Sam around and away from the window. He didn't know what he'd expected. He'd spent an hour alone, agonizing over Sara, more scared than he'd ever been, then had called Kathryn, knowing she'd want to come, needing some support himself.

What he doubted he could handle was time with Erin again. Exhausted from worry, he wrestled to keep his feelings at bay. "She's all right," he said to ease the worry from the faces of both women.

"Oh, thank God," Kathryn murmured, rushing to the bed. Without a look at him, Erin inched to the other side. Bending over Sara, she stroked her forehead.

Weary, Sam ran a hand across tired eyes, then set a foam cup of cold coffee on the small table near the door. "I'm glad you came." As Erin raised her head, he nodded. "Both of you." He'd said the words honestly. "She's been asking for you."

Staring down at Sara, so sweet, so innocent, so vulnerable, Erin felt her heart twist. "What happened?"

"The doctor said it was croup. They took an X-ray and are giving her antibiotics."

"How frightening for her." She looked back at him, at the strain etched in his face. "For you."

He'd never known such terror, prayed he never would again. "She's okay now. That's all that matters. She'll be glad you're here."

"Grandma. Aunt Erin."

At the soft, weak sound of her niece's voice, Erin whirled back to her and clutched her small hand. "I'm here."

"Will you stay with me?"

Kathryn blinked back tears and managed a tight-lipped smile. "We'll stay."

"Aunt Erin, you, too?"

She'd always said she'd only stay until Rory was clear. But she wasn't ready to leave. God, but she didn't want to leave. She took Sara's hand in hers, realizing she'd never planned to love Sam again or to fall in love with his daughter. The agony had been too immediate from her last loss, but here in the town she'd left so many years ago was everything she'd always wanted. "Oh, yes, Sara, I'll stay."

Helplessness from the past hours weakening him, Sam needed to get out of the room. He hated the emptiness shadowing him, the hurt still fresh inside him. "I'll get some coffee," he volunteered. Not waiting for their response, he strode out of the room and down the hall. More than coffee, he needed air.

Across Sara, Kathryn frowned with worry. "I'm sorry," she said softly.

"It's all right." Erin cradled Sara a moment longer. Easing Sara from her arms, she sent her mother a smile. "Wish me luck." She swung around and tore through the hospital hallway. Unmindful that she didn't have her coat, she rushed toward the exit, doubting he'd gone far. As he started to close the door, she yanked it back.

Sam balked. "What the hell's the matter with you?"

Chin up, she met the challenge in his eyes. "That's my question." Minus her jacket, Erin ignored the chill in the air as she marched outside ahead of him. Moonlight shone on the snow blanketing the courtyard.

"You shouldn't make that kind of promise to Sara," he said, using anger to keep needs away. "She'll expect you to keep it."

"I told her the truth." Wind whipped at her hair. "I couldn't leave her now. Or you," she said softly.

Damn, but he was aching to reach for her. That was the simple way. For Sara, he couldn't take it. He couldn't allow his own vulnerability to obliterate good sense. He relied on anger. "Why now? What's different?"

"Sam, please," she begged as he took a step to leave. "Don't turn away without listening." Shivering, Erin crossed her arms and hugged herself. For a long moment, she waited, but the rigid set of his back carried a clear message. Sensing she had to make the first move, she stepped closer to him. "Do you really think I'd believe Sara could take second place to anyone? Sam, she's beautiful. She's wonderful. I'll always cherish Lisa's memory, but I'd never expect any child to take the place of another."

In his heart, he never doubted she really cared about Sara. "I was angry. That's why I said that," he admitted.

"But you still think everything is about Sara, don't you?"

He was tired. He was in no mood for this.

She didn't need a response from him. His silence said it all. Impatience rippled through her. "I could lie but that would be dumb. If you want me to say I don't love your daughter, that's too bad. I do."

He dug a hand into his pants pocket. Why did he still want to say to hell with everything else and accept whatever she'd offer? She loved his child. That should be enough. God, but it wasn't.

"I love her as if she were my own child. But then you and she are a package deal, aren't you? And if I love her father then it makes sense I might love his daughter. Don't you know how much I want what you offered?"

Studying her, he narrowed his gaze. "Before, you couldn't say those words. Why now?"

Challenge darkened his eyes. When she was younger, she'd met and matched it. A warmth began to seep through her. She could win. He could. They all could, she realized in that one second. "You asked why I kept seeing you. I know now it was because I was falling in love with you again, but I didn't admit it to myself. I couldn't until I faced the past—the pain." She paused, but now wasn't the time to falter. "Sam, I loved Lisa so much, but I never grieved because I thought it would mean letting her go." She let out a long, steadying breath. "Grief stopped me from reaching out to you. If I let it go, I thought I'd lose her forever. I know now I was clinging to the sadness. That was wrong. It's the wonderful memories of Lisa I should treasure."

A trace of understanding in his eyes encouraged her, made her go on. "I didn't realize that my heart's been healing. Because of you, because of Sara. And I suppose I was afraid," she said softly. "Because to have a child, to have a family—with you—frightened me. I've had it, and I've lost it. Oh, Sam, you were offering me everything I'd ever wanted. Everything." She took a chance and stepped within inches of him. "And I couldn't accept it until I gave up the pain."

Shifting his stance, he looked away. Why had he assumed so much? Faced with such honesty from her, he had no choice but to match it. Too much pride—fear, too—had muddled him. Every other woman he'd loved had wanted something more. Because he'd expected her to be no different from them, he'd allowed a hint of doubt to become too important. "Damn fool."

Her head reared back. "Me?"

"No, me," he said softly. "I wasn't thinking straight. I began to believe that you were caught up in being around Sara, that I never mattered, that you saw me only as Sara's father."

At his discomfort, her heart opened further. "Oh, right." A touch of a smile tugging the corners of her lips, she grazed his cheek with her fingertips. "I just make love with you because then I might see Sara?"

He wished he didn't sound so idiotic suddenly.

"It's my fault, not yours," she said softly. "If I'd told you how I felt, you wouldn't have had doubts. Sam, I love you. Do you still care?"

He released a soft laugh and caught her to him. "I never stopped caring."

She didn't wait for him to say more. Her arms sliding around him, she raised her mouth to his. Long and deep, the kiss bound them to each other, carried a promise of tomorrow, of a future together.

"Are you freezing?" he murmured against her mouth.

She met his eyes and saw all the love she'd closed her mind to. Joy humming through her, she laughed. "No, I'm warm. Wonderfully warm."

Hand in hand, they strolled back to Sara's room.

Sara gave them a sleepy smile, but her blue eyes, so large in her pale face, turned on Erin. "Will you really stay?"

Erin winked at her mother before taking Sara's hand in hers. "I'm staying."

Sara's stare remained unwavering. "How long?"

"For as long as you want."

"Forever?"

Erin bent over and kissed her. "That's what your daddy said, too. So it looks like I have to stay." Erin watched Sara's smile widen. "We have to plan a wedding."

Sam saw the light he'd longed for come into his daughter's eyes.

"The three of us?" she asked excitedly.

Erin placed her hand on Sam's as he touched his daughter's hand. "We couldn't do it without you."

Chapter Thirteen

The two days Sara had spent in the hospital had seemed like an eternity to Sam. Now, watching Sara bound around her grandmother's living room, he had a hard time believing she'd ever been sick.

Head bent, she paused in coloring. "Will I be in the wedding?"

At the dining room table gathering dirty dishes, Erin smiled at Sam across the room. "You'll be one of the most important people. A flower girl."

Sara glowed. "And have a pretty dress?"

"The prettiest."

"And then we'll go on a honeymoon?"

"No, first we go on one," Sam cut in. He caught her and tossed her in the air and brought her down in a sweeping manner that stirred her giggle. "Then we'll come back and we'll all go on one."

"To Disneyland," she said, reminding them of their promise. "And..." She paused with the ringing of the telephone.

"I'll get it," Erin called out to her mother.

Sara tugged at Sam's hand. "Let's play Chutes and Ladders."

"I'll win," he said, dropping to the rug beside her.

"I'll win," she returned.

Erin reached for the telephone receiver. She was the one who'd really won, she decided before offering a greeting.

"Erin, where are you?" the caller asked demandingly.

She could imagine her agent tapping a pencil impatiently on her desk. "Lee, I left a message."

"Yes, something about getting married, but—"

"Lee, I'm sorry. I'm not coming."

"Now, you mean?"

"No, I'm staying here."

"Erin, this is your big chance. What more could you want?"

Nothing, she realized. Happiness filled her as she stared at Sam and Sara on the rug.

"Set up the board, Sara." Sam pushed to a stand and moved close to Erin. "Be sure," he said after she finished her conversation.

Her hip tightly pressed to his, gently she brushed a finger down his jaw. "Be sure about what? Loving you? Marrying you? Being Sara's mother?"

"Giving it all up."

She noted the concern clouding his eyes. Coiling her arms around his neck, she swayed into him. She was gaining far more than she was giving up. "What choice did I have? The two of you ganged up on me."

At the tease in her voice, he grinned. "Irresistible, aren't we?"

"Irresistible," she murmured against his lips.

* * * * *

Get Ready to be Swept Away by
Silhouette's Spring Collection

Abduction
&
Seduction

These passion-filled stories explore both the dangerous
desires of men and the seductive powers of women.
Written by three of our most celebrated authors, they are
sure to capture your hearts.

Diana Palmer
Brings us a spin-off of her Long, Tall Texans series

Joan Johnston
Crafts a beguiling Western romance

Rebecca Brandewyne
New York Times bestselling author
makes a smashing contemporary debut

Available in March at your favorite retail outlet.

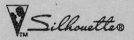

Silhouette®

MILLION DOLLAR SWEEPSTAKES (III)

Silhouette celebrates motherhood in May with...

Debbie Macomber
Jill Marie Landis
Gina Ferris Wilkins

in

Three
Mothers
& a Cradle

Join three award-winning authors in this
beautiful collection you'll treasure forever.
The same antique, hand-crafted cradle
connects these three heartwarming romances,
which celebrate the joys and excitement of
motherhood. Makes the perfect gift for yourself
or a loved one!

A special celebration of love,

Only from

V *Silhouette*®
™

—where passion lives.

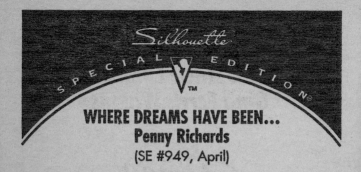

Silhouette
SPECIAL EDITION™

WHERE DREAMS HAVE BEEN...
Penny Richards
(SE #949, April)

Someone had taken Julee Sutherland's child. And only her enigmatic neighbor, Dane Collier, could help find the missing baby. But that meant using his special powers to tap into long-buried dreams and memories of the past—that linked him and Julee together...forever.

That SPECIAL Woman!

She had the courage to follow her convictions.... Would she be rewarded with the man of her dreams?

Don't miss *Where Dreams Have Been...*by Penny Richards, available in April!

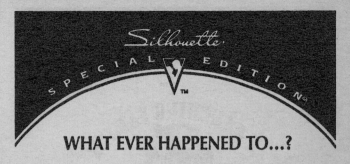

Silhouette

SPECIAL EDITION™

WHAT EVER HAPPENED TO...?

Have you been wondering when much-loved characters will finally get their
own stories? Well, have we got a lineup for you! Silhouette Special Edition is
proud to present a **Spin-off Spectacular!** Be sure to catch these exciting
titles from some of your favorite authors:

Jake's Mountain (March, SE #945) Jake Harris never met anyone as
stubborn—or as alluring—as Dr. Maggie Matthews, in Christine Flynn's
latest novel, a spin-off to *When Morning Comes* (SE #922).

Rocky Mountain Rancher (April , SE #951) Maddy Henderson must decide if
sexy loner Luther Ward really *was* after her ranch, or truly falling for her, in
Pamela Toth's tie-in to *The Wedding Knot* (SE #905).

Don't miss these wonderful titles, only for our readers—only from
Silhouette Special Edition!

Silhouette

SPECIAL EDITION™

A RANCHING FAMILY

Though scattered by years and tears, the Heller clan
share mile-deep roots in one Wyoming ranch—and a
single talent for lassoing hearts!

Meet another member of the Heller clan in
Victoria Pade's
BABY MY BABY
(SE #946, March)

The ranching spirit coursed through
Beth Heller's veins—as did the passion she
felt for her proud Sioux husband, Ash Blackwolf. Yet
their marriage was in ashes. Only the
unexpected new life growing within Beth could bring
them together again....

Don't miss **BABY MY BABY,** the next installment of
Victoria Pade's series,
A RANCHING FAMILY, available in March!
And watch for Jackson Heller's story,
COWBOY'S KISS, coming in July...only from
Silhouette Special Edition!

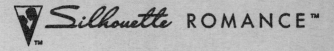
Silhouette ROMANCE™

Arriving in April from Silhouette Romance...

Bundles
of Joy

Six bouncing babies. Six unforgettable love stories.

Join Silhouette Romance as we present these heartwarming tales
featuring the joy that only a baby can bring!

THE DADDY PROJECT by Suzanne Carey
THE COWBOY, THE BABY AND THE RUNAWAY BRIDE
by Lindsay Longford
LULLABY AND GOODNIGHT by Sandra Steffen
ADAM'S VOW by Karen Rose Smith
BABIES INC. by Pat Montana
HAZARDOUS HUSBAND by Christine Scott

Don't miss out on these BUNDLES OF JOY—only from Silhouette Romance.
Because sometimes, the smallest packages can lead to the biggest surprises!

And be sure to look for additional BUNDLES OF JOY
titles in the months to come.

THE MACKADE BROTHERS

the exciting new series by
New York Times bestselling author

Nora Roberts

The MacKade Brothers—looking for trouble,
and always finding it. Now they're on a collision
course with love. And it all begins with

**THE RETURN OF RAFE MACKADE
(Intimate Moments #631, April 1995)**

The whole town was buzzing. Rafe MacKade
was back in Antietam, and that meant only one
thing—there was bound to be trouble....

Be on the lookout for the next book in the
series, **THE PRIDE OF JARED MACKADE—
Silhouette Special Edition's 1000th Book!**
It's an extraspecial event not to be missed,
coming your way in December 1995!

THE MACKADE BROTHERS—these sexy, trouble-
loving men will be heading out to you in alternate books from Silhouette Intimate Moments
and Silhouette Special Edition.
Watch out for them!

NRTITLE